CW00338908

Saga ©

THE
DUKE TARSET

Levi Samuel

PUBLISHING

ELDARLANDS©

THE DUKE TARSET
Eldarlands Publishing
Copyright © 2015-2019

The story, cover art, and illustrations by Levi Samuel.

Genre: Fantasy / Time Travel

ISBN-13: 978-1-950541-13-3

Find all the author's projects at http://www.LeviSamuel.com

This book is dedicated to you, my dear reader.
Your interest is what allows me to do what I love.
For that, you have my eternal thanks.

Contents

Prologue

The needle-like tip flowed gracefully across the rough parchment. All things considered it should have been no big deal, but the wood pulp was by far outdated compared to the ornate writing device. Commonly scribed with quill and ink, the bulbous blots were meant to be absorbed by the thick sheet. As it were, the thin markings had to be written slow if the conservative contraption was to function as intended. Such was to be expected when pairing superior tools to archaic practice.

The fountain pen, so it had been called by those more familiar with its use, was but one of many items found within the Hall of Guardians. In fact, every item that had been lost throughout all of eternity had ended up here. Loose coins of every era that had fallen between the cushions, random guitar picks, pocketknives dulled with use but oddly misplaced, and a great many socks, most of them the left from a time when socks were directional, comprised the bulk of these trinkets.

The Hall of Guardians was the only structure built into the realm of Purgatory. Some called it the void, others named it the nothing, or the empty. Regardless of its name, it was the one place that existed between time. A place the Duke Tarset call home. And it was the easiest place in existence to jump between worlds.

Fenlara smiled at the words scrolling the page. They were far from anything considered a masterpiece, but she'd always prided herself on being educated. Even if that education were limited to a certain world view. It was a view that had been turned upside down over the past few months, but as her horizons broadened, a world of knowledge previously unknown came to her.

The world was a much larger place than she could have ever imagined. She'd seen other places before. More than most as it were. The limitations were nearly nonexistent. She'd seen things and been places that most could never dream about. That wasn't to say her job was easy. Most days it was downright hard. But now that she was here, she wouldn't trade it for the world. If anything, she found it the most conventional afterlife she could have hoped for.

The thought made her pause a moment. Staring longingly at her combination of scribbles that passed for writing, barely legible to anyone but herself, she questioned the word. *Afterlife?* She hadn't died, and therefore by definition she had to be alive. *Could a living being experience afterlife?* When she accepted the job her life had not ceased. Rather, she had ascended. All in her station were. It was the only way to harness the powers required to perform their job. But did that mean she was dead? Or simply in another state of existence? In a way that's all death was. So, had her ascension actually been her death, or something less daunting?

Shaking her head, confusion growing by the moment, Fenlara began to read what she'd written moments before. It was pointless writing it down. No one else would ever read it, but it helped to comprehend this new world she was learning. And so much of it there was.

Time is a funny thing. It moves both linear and circular, which perplexes most observers. In fact, the easiest way to understand its functionality is to imagine a series of overlapping loops, intersecting here and there. You can enter or exit at any crossover. And if you stick around long enough, you can witness it repeat itself. But there's one element that baffles even those of us who work within it. That element is known as the paradox.

There are many kinds of paradoxes. Most are time distortions caused by those who misuse it. Actually, to a degree, all paradoxes are caused this way. There are however a select few that are required to keep time flowing as intended. These, at least in every case I've learned of, are called bootstrap paradoxes.

They earned their name because it's like trying to lift yourself off the ground by your own bootstraps. The competing forces of personal weight against personal strength will typically result in a stalemate. But when you include the outside force of time to the equation, in rare cases, you'll defy gravity. Hypothetically speaking of course, about the gravity, not time. Please allow me an example as I fear I haven't explained myself well enough.

Let's say there were a tyrannical god who washed over the mortal realms in hopes of eliminating every living being. This god met his downfall against a powerful mortal. The mortal goes on to become a god himself, only to discover some millennia later that he was in fact the same god he defeated so many years prior. During his conquest to rid the world of life he is defeated by his younger self, which restarts the cycle yet again.

This is a bootstrap paradox. I suppose in a simpler form I could have posed the age-old question between the chicken and the egg. But if we delve a little deeper, we could also ask, was this mortal originally the same being who became the god? Or was it always this way? And if so, how did he come to godhood in the first place? Why would he allow himself to be defeated if he knew it was coming? It creates more questions than answers.

I can't speak in confidence to either regard. Though I can say, in many cases, the first and original encounter would typically be two separate beings whose fate became intertwined during their battle. The mortal claims the mantle of god, and therefore seals himself into an indefinite loop where he must face himself twice in his existence. It's a question of cause and effect. A time loop which has no true ending, nor beginning. But it will always flow linear.

This is why the concept of time is so difficult to understand. The trick is to realize that there are no beginnings. And there are no ends. It will always flow the same direction, and with proper understanding and skill it can be navigated with near perfect precision.

Once you understand these fundamentals, time makes a lot more sense. Though I can't claim the same about your other perceptions. I know mine have become a bit skewed lately. But if you're reading this, I'm sure you're wondering, 'How would I know?'. Time is a tricky thing and without some form of credentials I could be some random nobody rambling on about my thoughts. This however, is not the case.

My name is Fenlara of Winstead, once a cleric of Ozmodius, now a Duke Tarset. But I'm willing to bet you've never heard of that, nor me for that matter, so I suppose that does little to strengthen my testimony. I suppose the only way to truly enlighten you is to give a little history.

Before the dukes, there was a god. Or three, actually. You know what? I'm just going to start the story at the beginning. Time is too complicated to start at the midway point and hope you're able to follow. But then again, we've already established there are no true beginnings, so really, we're wasting our time here even trying to explain it.

Time is a construct. Like the elements; fire, water, air, and so on, it has always and will always exist. There are some places outside of time, but even that's misleading. Time is still present in these places, it simply doesn't move. That can be good when you're not restricted by its flow. It's less beneficial when you are. That said, before time was regulated and the gods came to power there were three who tamed the universe. This is another paradox in itself but I don't wish to open that can of worms.

Ozmodius claimed the aspect of time. Osirus became death. And Izaryle created life. I'm probably getting a bit ahead of myself, but you need to know this to follow the story.

A great many things happened which led to the God War. And at some point along the way, Izaryle went mad. She led her children against the remaining gods and their followers but was eventually defeated. Her children were banished or killed, and she was imprisoned far beyond the known realms. I bet I just blew your mind there. Most people seem to believe Izaryle was a man. That's the funny thing about gods. Their gender is irrelevant. When they present themselves, they do so in whatever capacity they choose.

Anyway, they locked her away. That would have been great had everything gone as planned. But gods are not infallible. They are not all knowing, despite some claims as such. And just like mortals, gods can make mistakes. In fact, if my time as a duke has taught me anything, gods aren't gods at all. At least not in the way I believed in my younger years. A god is nothing more than a useless title bestowed by a lesser being. The relationship between god and mortal is similar to that of mortal and ant. Both are aware of the other's existence, but rarely do they interact unless they manage to find themselves in a place they ought not be.

That's where people like me come in.

I'm a Duke Tarset. Like hours in the day, there are twelve of us who regulate time. We keep things flowing smoothly during Ozmodius' god-sleep. Time is exhausting after all. I'm willing to bet I'd need a nap if I were to witness every second of every minute for all eternity in an infinite loop of endless possibilities. Just the mere thought makes me sleepy, and I'm conditioned for such. Of course, I don't see all. Simply the parts I'm involved with. And that's what I'm here to talk about...

5

Every clock in existence struck the hour in unison creating a chorus of chimes, gongs, beeps, peeps, and cuckoos.

The sudden alarm caused Fenlara to jump. The pages of her journal clapped together. She stared in disbelief, her nose wrinkled in annoyance. "Oh, fiddle sticks!" Carefully, she reopened the leather-wrapped book, inspecting the smudged writing. The ink was still wet, though the unexpected closure had thinned it considerably. But that also meant the words were no longer legible, not that there was much hope of that to begin with.

A smile crept to her lips, being a duke had its perks after all. Fenlara waved her hand over the damaged pages, tapping into her newly acquired abilities. Her fingers moved in unison, contorting as if tuning an unseen instrument.

The ink began to boil from the thick fibers, pooling into the crude lettering that had previously adorned the page. Content with its legibility, she released the minor alteration and watched the ink soak in once again.

The alarms continued to chime, demanding attention.

A deep sigh escaped her and she glanced around to the millions of time pieces comprising the walls in the Hall of Guardians. They only sounded when there was an abnormality, disturbance, or tear in the fabric of time. Usually, it was something small: a kid abandoning his dreams after a particularly difficult day, the accidental mishap which slipped through the cracks, or the underestimation of powers beyond control. Regardless of severity, it was Fenlara's job, as well as the other dukes, to ensure the abnormality was swiftly and completely mended. Only then could time return to its usual flow.

"Yes, yes, I hear you. I'll get on it in a moment!"

As if in response, the clocks fell silent at once.

Fenlara reached into a small bronze dish at the side of her desk and gathered a handful of pounce. Sprinkling it over the pages, she watched the excess ink dry and closed the book. Picking herself up, the irony of her actions was not lost. She'd used time to correct a mistake, however trivial that mistake was. The vast majority of paradoxes were created the same way. The only difference was she worked outside of time, whereas most others did not. It was also somewhat amusing that she'd taken the time to fix her book when something that could potentially end the world awaited her attention. But such was the life of a duke. Her world had become one big balancing act, holding one catastrophe at bay with another, all the while dangling a spare apocalypse in her pocket for good measure. Afterall, the end of the world was never more than a few small decisions away.

Laying her book upon the desk, Fenlara stood. It was time to go to work.

Getting dressed took little more than a thought. The flowing robes she wore in her off time were gone, replaced by a layer of clothing unlike anything found on the mortal plane. The dark fibers flowed like cloth but were hard as steel. Platemail layered over that, matte and black. An hourglass was embedded into the left of her breastplate, just visible under the shoulder pauldron.

Thousands of tiny granules of sand flowed against gravity, collecting in the top bulb, never to fill. Upon her left hip, a bastard sword hung sheathed, made of the same material as her armor. She didn't particularly care for the blade, preferring the use of spells and magic, but it was the ceremonious weapon of the Duke Tarset and their god before them. If nothing else, it was an intimidating instrument and good to have when such need arose. As her mentor would say, 'Hope for the best, prepare for the worst!'.

Dressed and ready, Fenlara inspected her garb. She felt a bit silly in such heavy armor, though its physical weight was next to

7

nothing. It was more the idea of her appearance in accordance with who she was. Despite some of the jokes that had been made at her expense during the Demon Wars, she was far from a damsel in distress. In fact, combat was no stranger. She'd been involved in numerous battles, some more dire than others. In many cases, it was the experience of those battles that led to her position among the dukes.

Dismissing her personal feelings about the uniform, Fenlara approached the only portion of the wall not covered in clocks. It was reflective and tall, a mirror, serving as the doorway to all other places in and out of purgatory. Placing her hand over the hourglass in her armor, she stepped through.

Chapter 1

Gasping breaths echoed through the dark room. Fenlara had difficulty catching her breath. She was dying. The question was, how much longer could she last?

Her eyes had grown accustomed to the sparse light. It entered from a small opening in the ceiling of the grand tent. The rest was obstructed by a metal flue exhausting from the stove in the corner. The burning wood did little to warm the room, despite its billowing flames. Between her condition, and the general cold seeping from the ground and beneath the thin canvas walls, she couldn't feel any warmth.

Her fingers squished in the soggy mixture of grass and dirt beneath her. She found herself wishing it was just melted snow, but she knew that wasn't the case. Sure, snow had been a part of it, but the bulk of the moisture was an excessive amount of spilled blood, much of it hers.

Despite the cold, a boiling sweat was beading across her forehead and down her back. It made her shiver, though she wasn't sure if it was from the temperature or something else. She wasn't sure of much anymore.

There was so much blood, slick and sticky. It clung to her hands, soaked into her clothes. Her armor was useless to protect against it. If anything, it was little more than a metal casket where she would wither away until nothing was left.

Hatred burned inside her. She wanted revenge against the people who had done this too her. A quick and painless death was too good for them. Fenlara gritted her teeth, letting another painful moment pass her by. All she could do was wait. Wait for death. Wait for it all to be over.

It was amusing, though she didn't feel much like laughing about it. The threat of extinction, the end of existence, all of it was upon her, and not just her own. All of time and space was at risk and somehow she'd found herself at the root of it.

Bile forced its way from her mouth, expelling stomach acid and bloody saliva into the mixture of dirt, snow, and blood. Fenlara doubled in pain. It wouldn't be much longer now.

Staring helpless at the other bodies lying about the room, Fenlara felt for them. At least the man hadn't felt much of anything before he passed. It had been quick. Gruesome, but quick. The other one wasn't so fortunate. She was bleeding out, though occasionally her whimpers could still be heard. It was a painful way to go, but she'd faced it like a champion.

In a weird way, it had been those occasional sobs that kept her going. Though it had been a while since she heard the last one. Fenlara wondered if she was finally gone.

Her body doubled, muscles spasming and contorting at weird angles. Her breath quickened. The pain grew to a near constant. Sweating, panting, straining for strength, she fought with everything she had, but it wasn't enough. Fenlara collapsed, her face pressing into the churned and bloody earth. Rolling her head, she set eyes on her murderer, strolling away. He was content. He'd taken pleasure in her torment, and she was helpless to do anything about it. Though one thing was certain. This was a hell of a way to go out, not swinging but bringing all of existence with her.

Chapter II

"I can't do this!" Fenlara declared, pleading her case to the Duke Tarset.

"Yes, you can. Remember, it's not about the object. It's about everything else. Try again." Trendal gestured to the man standing at the end of the dimly lit alley way.

Exhaling sharply, Fenlara squared off and prepared herself. According to the duke, this little exercise would become a second nature. Thus far it had proved anything but. Giving a nod, she fought the anxiety building within her. She'd relived this moment more times than she could count. Though each time it caught her off guard.

An ear shattering bang erupted from the miniature cannon locked in the man's grip. It was a simple device, handle, body, and muzzle. It reminded her of a crossbow, though much smaller, and it was the concealed canisters inside that projected its ammunition rather than the flex of a bow.

A flash of fire and smoke preluded the sight of the tiny bolt. It wasn't much larger than a pebble, though clearly made of metal. Fenlara watched the projectile escape the end of the snubbed tube. It had taken many attempts, but she could at least see it now. Before, it had moved so quickly she'd never seen it coming. It was slow progress, but progress nonetheless. Though it posed a question. Was it her perceptions that had changed, or was she finally learning how to slow time?

Straining, she forced the metallic rock coming toward her from her mind. Replaying the duke's words, she thought aloud.

"It's not about the object. It's about everything else. What does that even mean?"

Her focus shifted to the man. He was of a grungy sort. His pants were dirty and torn. He wore a stained gray shirt which covered the same as a tunic, though its design was vastly different. This was a thick but soft material and had a hood similar to that of a winter cloak, though it clearly wasn't that either. She'd heard the name once, but it slipped her mind. It was something simple and she remembered thinking it odd for something so strange. Of course, everything here was strange.

The buildings were made of liquified stone which became hard once poured. Glass was smooth and so clear you could see through it as if it wasn't really there. The wagons moved fast and didn't rely on horses, though still were powered by horsepower. Lamps were fireless, and there was so much noise she couldn't hear herself think. The duke had promised strange and wonderful things. This was clearly both, though she couldn't say for certain if she liked it.

Fenlara was running out of time. The bolt was upon her. She winced, feeling it make contact. Its concave head pressed into her chest, imploding upon itself. The metal was beginning to flatten, its powerful force shoving her backward. The pain was nearly unbearable, ebbing throughout her body. Had it been moving any faster, or she any slower, it would have tore a hole straight through her. Though if she delayed much longer, it was going to do that anyway. Whether she'd managed to increase her perceptions, or slow the bolt, neither meant anything if she couldn't learn to interact in such a state.

Sighing his impatience, Trendal raised his hand. The bullet came to a sudden stop. Taking a deep breath, he exhaled, shaking his head. He was growing tired of seeing the same thing time and again. She was learning. That was a plus, but it was much slower than he'd intended. Waving his hand, the bullet moved backward, retracting itself. Flying through the air, the broken sound waves inverted, pulling themselves together. Fire and smoke rolled toward the short barrel, climbing inside as the bullet joined them. The man's finger released the trigger and he froze, unwittingly awaiting time to resume.

For the hundred and twenty sixth time everything was where it had been. Trendal approached the newly elected duke. Placing his hands on her shoulders, he stared into her for a long moment. He could see she was frustrated. She had every right to be. But she also had to learn. Trial by fire was always the fastest method of teaching, provided the student didn't get burned.

Trendal had selected this exact time and place for a number of reasons. First off, it was convenient. He'd been on assignment here, which worked perfectly for training the new pup. His second and third reasons were more lesson based.

Fenlara was a bit of a heavy-handed caster. He knew that the moment they'd met. She preferred spells over tactics, which wasn't a bad thing, but she had yet to take into account her surroundings. Magic was alive. It thrived in some places better than others. And this was one of the hardest places in the known world to cast. Between the excessive city noise and mass amounts of light pollution, not to mention the rarity of magic in this age, she'd have to step up her game if she was to pull it off. She'd have to learn to adapt her spellwork or find an alternative. Thus far she hadn't managed either.

Additionally, had it not been for their presence, the mugger would have murdered two people this night and left a child scarred for life. They would never know who saved them, and they'd never wonder about it. Fenlara had to understand this was a thankless job. Most of her deeds would go unnoticed and underappreciated. She would have to find her own way to deal with that. The quicker it happened, the better off she'd be.

And lastly, his final reason was of a more personal nature. This city was home to the best pizza across the known universe and all of time. If only she'd apply herself and learn this simple ability, he'd already be there enjoying a pie or three.

The duke forced a reassuring smile. It seemed she was going to be more receptive to a nurturing approach. "Okay, when you slow time, what is it you're thinking about?" He didn't have to ask the question. She hadn't learned to regulate her thoughts yet. To a psionist it was no different than someone who verbalized every detail that crossed their mind. But he wasn't going to tell her that. She had enough to learn for now.

"The bang makes me jump every time. I see the flash and I know I have less than a heartbeat before it's going to hit me. My mind clears and I think if I can slow it, I'll have more time to figure out how to stop it. But it never stops."

"I see your problem. Okay, I want you to try something different. I want you to forget about the gun, the bang, and all of it. Instead, imagine a flowing stream. Do you have it?" She did.

"Yes."

"Okay, can you see the current washing across the rocks, flowing faster in some places and slower in others? Do you see the water swirling where the two come together, creating little white capped rapids where its steep?"

"Yes."

"Do you hear the subtle roar, trickling down the cascading stone?"

"I do."

"Keep that thought in your mind. See it. Hear it. Let it replace your distractions. And when you hear nothing but the flowing water, I want you to make it stop. Pause it completely. Nothing can move. If you see a leaf floating on the surface, it becomes frozen. That bird flying overhead can't flap its wings, but it also can't fall from the sky. Everything is silent. Everything is still. It's all under your command. You, a Duke Tarset, are the only one in existence that can move through this picture. Can you do that?"

"I'll try."

A soft chuckle escaped the duke. "Do or do not. There is no try!"

"What's that mean?"

"I'm sure you'll find out for yourself one of these days. Are you ready?"

"I guess."

"Do you have your stream?"

"Yes"

"Open your eyes."

Fenlara did as commanded. Her vision filled with the shiny metal rock frozen in the air. It was surrounded by flame and a few grains of dark sand that hadn't yet burned. Not so much as a sound could be heard. And best of all, her river was still stationary. "Am I doing this?"

"You are."

Fenlara jumped rapidly, squealing her excitement. "I did it! I did it!" Approaching the bullet, having just exited the gun, she inspected it freely for the first time. It had been one thing when it was approaching her, but now she could move around it. "Can I touch it?"

"You can. It's no different than picking up the leaf frozen in your stream."

Carefully, Fenlara placed her finger and thumb on either side of the bullet and plucked it from the air.

"Be careful when you release your hold. It only lasts a short while and you have to remember the force that propelled it still exists. Make sure it's facing a safe direction before your control wains."

Nodding her understanding, Fenlara redirected the bullet to embed itself into the bricked wall running the length of the alley.

She could feel a tension growing in the air around her. It was pulling at her, getting tighter by the moment. Glancing in all directions, she could see bits of static sparking here and there. It felt sticky, getting warmer moment by moment. She poked her hand into one of the unusual pockets, seeing it slip from view. "Is this how I tell how much time is left?"

Trendal smiled. "Yes. Time wants to flow. The longer you hold it the more it backs up. It's like trying to restrain a river. You can dam it, but it's going to build up. When the levee breaks, you'll flood everything on the other side. Try to keep that from happening. It's hard to play catch when both sides of the field are muddy."

"I don't know what that means."

"If you cause a flood you have to do your regular job on top of fixing all the things you broke."

"Oh, okay. So, what else do we do?"

"Well, first you're going to want to pull your hand out of that timestream. You never know when those are going to close and it sucks trying to find your own missing pieces. After that, we go get some pizza!"

Chapter III

No! She would not go out that way. She was a fighter! It was time to fight! Fenlara pulled herself up. She was a Duke Tarset after all, a keeper of time, a protector of realms. She'd been a powerful force long before she knew what a duke was. Just because they'd stolen that power away from her didn't mean she was helpless.

Reaching out, Fenlara pushed through the pain. The pounding inside her head was somehow lessened by the threat of imminent death. Her grip wrapped around her fleeing murderer. It wasn't so much as her physical grip. No, she was much too weak for that. This was her mental grip, her psionics. She pushed past the demonic blood they'd pumped into her veins, straining to keep her focus. Locking onto him, she crawled to her knees. Squeezing with all her might, his arms slapped to his sides. He was the helpless one now. Fenlara lifted him off the ground, turning him to face her. She got to her feet, staggering ever closer. She wanted to stare into his eyes. He was an evil man and he needed to be punished.

Damion struggled against the unseen bonds. Despite his confinement, a confident smirk remained present. "Please!" He chuckled through her crushing grip, spitting blood from his wicked mouth. "Ya really think a few lingering powers mean anything to the will of my Lord? Kill me a thousand times over, each time, my master will resurrect me, for it's already too late to stop what's been set in motion. As we speak, Ozmodius falls. And ya don't have the time or power to do anything about it."

He was right. She was weak, and as soon as time realized what had happened, it'd catch up to her and she'd cease to exist. But that wasn't grounds for letting this evil creature live. He'd already done so much damage. What would he do in a world unchecked by the dukes? No, he had to die!

Squeezing with all her might, Fenlara listened to the snaps and pops echo within his crushed body. Releasing her grip, Damion collapsed to the floor, little more than a pile of skin and meat, though he was still alive. She prayed it would last quite some time, though it was doubtful. At the very least, his final moments would be little more than unbearable anguish. It was better than he deserved.

Fenlara limped to the crumbled woman lying not far from her. She could still see faint movement, though how she hadn't perished long ago was a mystery of its own. There was so much blood, and the wound would never heal without magical treatment. Unfortunately, that was beyond her ability at the moment. "I'm sorry this happened to you. It was not part of your timeline, but that doesn't mean it has to be final."

Lifting the battery in her hand, Fenlara inspected the glowing window. She hadn't been trained in its use, but she couldn't allow the stolen magics to remain trapped. They were too dangerous. Twisting the cap, she opened the device allowing the power to escape. One after another Fenlara pulled the canisters from the satchel near the pile of Damion.

The freed energy swirled in the air around her, glowing like an aurora in the sky. Much of it disappeared into the ether, but just enough found its way into her. Opening a doorway into the timestream, Fenlara grabbed hold of the dying woman. It was risky, but what choice did she have? The other dukes were gone. If Damion had been telling the truth, she was the last. If she didn't act, they would all be dead, existence along with them.

It was a warm and comfortable feeling. She hadn't expected that. Fenlara felt the energy resonate between them. Blinding blue light filled her vision, erupting between their touch. Tendrils of temporal power jumped between them and the doorway.

Everything was so bright, blinding and hot. It roared, drowning out all other sound. The timestream split open, swallowing the entire room. Everything was gone, everything except Fenlara and her ward.

Pulling the girl tight, the duke wrapped her arms around her chest. The last thing she wanted was to lose her before they saw the end of this, whatever that outcome would be.

Pieces of time flew past, traveling quicker than most were capable of seeing. Fenlara recognized them for what they were. She was in a time vortex, only none of this was linear. It was as if all of time swarmed around them, chaotic and tangled. The timestreams she'd grown familiar with were small by comparison, narrow tunnels that were organized and direct. This was something else, something raw and powerful.

The forceful currents ripped her this way and that, throwing her through solid objects and dragging her under oceans. There was no up, there was no down. Everything was simply there. And all she could do was hang on for the ride. But that didn't mean navigation wouldn't work just the same.

Willing herself, Fenlara held tight to the young woman. They came to a stop, floating between nothing and everything. For the first time since this nightmare had begun, there was hope. Now all they had to do was find somewhere safe to heal their wounds. With renewed confidence, Fenlara willed them forward and they started to move.

It was tricky at first. Navigating a timestream was like riding a waterfall through a drain and into a pipe. Every twist and turn was predetermined, eventually leading to the exit point regardless of the quality of ride. She'd learned the tricks to do it safely. This was something different. More akin to trying to surf a tidal wave through a ruptured dam, all the while dodging obstacles and avoiding destruction along the way. The flow ripped her back and forth, carrying her through places and times unknown. Flashes of sight zipped by. She passed through land masses and stars, living creatures and dead worlds. None of it looked familiar.

Straining to keep her grip, to both sanity and her ward, a beacon illuminated through the chaos. If she could reach it, maybe there was some lingering hope after all.

Fighting to keep her will, Fenlara rolled and ducked, kicked and dove, making her way toward the source. She smashed into a wall of energy and suddenly her movement ceased. She hit the ground hard, bouncing and rolling across the floor. She slammed into the wall and came to an abrupt stop. The impact was far from pleasant, though it was nothing compared to the pain she'd already endured. If anything she found it a welcome comfort. After everything she'd endured during her captivity, and the multiple collisions since, it was a reminder that she was still alive.

Fenlara groaned and opened her eyes. She wanted nothing more than to lay there a moment longer. Unfortunately, she didn't have that luxury. All of existence hung in the balance. If not from her paradox, then from whoever this *Master* was.

Subtle light filled her vision and familiar sights began to take focus. Fenlara sat up rapidly, staring longingly at the picture of a turnip mounted above her bed. Somehow, against all odds, she'd managed to find her way to the Hall of Guardians.

Chapter IV

The surface shimmered, swallowing her like water. Darkness enveloped her for the briefest moment, instantly replaced by blinding light.

Fenlara shielded her eyes, allowing them a moment to adjust. She was standing in a city, though it was unlike the cities she was used to.

Everything moved so fast and the people seemed so busy. The sun was much closer than she remembered, which accounted for the heat.

Glancing at the people around her, Fenlara realized how out of place she was. Swords and armor were not common in this age. Instead, they relied on thin light colored clothing, and their weapon of choice had become these plastic rectangles with moving pictures inside them. She knew they were called cell phones, though the term seemed to be a catchall rather than a specific name. The last time she'd encountered them, they were these big blocky looking devices with large buttons and long antennas. Now, they didn't appear to have more than a couple buttons around the sides and people interacted with the pictures instead.

Fenlara's armor melded away, replaced by a thin overshirt made of a mesh material. Beneath that, a floral shirt clung tight to her form, and a pair of entirely too short for comfort tan shorts took the place of her dark breeches. She wasn't overly happy with the clothing her adaptive camouflage provided. And while she had control over it, she matched the people around her. That was more important than comfort. Though the shoes she genuinely liked. They had far more cushion than the boots of her age.

Alarms sounded in the distance, growing closer by the moment, though they were unlike any she'd heard before. These were rhythmic and loud. It bounced off the towering buildings of glass and stone. From here, it wasn't far to a grand ocean that disappeared into the distance, though it was more crowded than any sea she'd seen. Massive boats littered the surface, though an extreme few seemed to rely on sails to propel them.

A flash of light caught Fenlara's attention, reminding her what she had to do.

Red and blue strobes danced atop an army of horseless wagons. They'd soon be upon her, but it wasn't the screaming chariots that demanded her attention. It was the larger wagon they were chasing, colored two shades of brown.

Searching her surroundings, Fenlara spotted a chariot of her own. It was blue, shiny, and somehow reminded her of a turnip. If that wasn't a sign, she didn't know what was.

Approaching the strange contraption, car, the word appeared in her memory, she was surprised to find the door locked. Her nose wrinkled in contempt. Now was not the time for such annoyances.

Taking into account her place in time, Fenlara attuned herself to the lingering energies of the world around her. They were dormant here and hard to grab, but she'd spent months practicing the technique.

Focusing them, using her innate power as the catalyst, Fenlara shaped the spell and released a controlled wave into the door.

With an audible click, a small stick popped up behind the glass window and the door came open. Fenlara pulled it to her and climbed inside. The engine roared to life no sooner than the door closed.

She stared at the complicated machine for a long moment. It was filled with odd levers and strange knobs. How she missed the days when all you had to do was guide the reins and the horse would obey.

Hitting one of the levers, a set of sticks rotated across the front window. Trying to shut it off, she hit a button that made the most obnoxious, yet unintimidating beep. Different knobs did different things, but the strangest of them all was a little button that made unexpected sounds and voices blast from the walls. No matter what she said, they didn't seem to hear her. A few arrows later, the voices went away and a rhythmic tune reminiscent of music began to play. This was something far removed from the bards of her age but she kind of liked it.

Willing the car to move, Fenlara wrapped her hands around the firm yet flexible wheel. "Go!" She commanded, releasing her power. The car began to lift off the ground. "No, not like that!" It dropped roughly. "Back up!" There was no response. Sighing, she inspected the controls all around her. Surely one of them would make it move.

A stick, protruding from the compartment between the seats, caught her attention. It had an odd combination of letters and numbers, but the orange line pointed at the large 'P'. Pushing the button on the handle, the stick gave a little play but held fast.

Exhaling through her nose, she stole a glance at her approaching target. She didn't have time for this.

Placing her hand on the dash, Fenlara let the temporal power flow through her. Memories came into her mind, though they were not her own. She witnessed the car's creation, its first drive, even the spilled food that remained trapped between the rear seats. Every moment of its existence, and the parts beforehand were now as much a part of her as her own life. But more importantly, she now knew how to drive it.

Pressing the wide pedal at her feet, she squeezed the button and moved the lever from 'P' to 'R'. Letting the pedal up, the car slowly began to move. Fenlara rotated the wheel, angling the nose toward the road she needed. Taking a deep breath, she shifted to 'D', and pressed the narrow pedal as far as it would go.

A sudden crash shook the carriage, throwing her sideways. An explosion of dust filled the air and a series of white bags tore through the dark gray material covering the wheel, dash, and side posts.

Staring through the broken glass, Fenlara could see two men in the large brown wagon. Their faces were obscured by black masks, leaving nothing but their eyes visible. They were too busy to pay much attention to her. The adjoined vehicles slid across the pavement and collided into a leafless tree with wires attached to the top.

This was it. This was why she was here. She had to stop the brown metal wagon. Time would do the rest.

Tailoring the power to her needs, Fenlara opened a doorway around her. The broken metal and plastics faded and she materialized a few blocks away. Looking down the hill, she could see the aftermath of her interference. It wasn't always a sight she cherished but it was what she had to do.

Several pops echoed from the crash. Gunfire, she recalled. Between the panicked screams and commotion, she wanted nothing more than to return and stop all of it. People killing other people was stupid. But it seemed a commonality regardless of what time she was in. She'd had to participate in her own share of battles more times than she cared to admit. It didn't make it any easier. And standing here watching it happen didn't help matters. She'd done her job. It was time to move on.

Closing her eyes, Fenlara let the power encase her and she materialized far from the gunshots. She could still hear sirens, but they were far off, likely not even the same ones. That's what she told herself anyway.

A different siren filled the air and Fenlara's attention fell solely on a large colosseum. The construction was similar to that of the gladiator fights she saw in Rome. Though the noise from this place was much different. The mob was chanting, not for blood but for sport.

The energies wrapped around her and Fenlara found herself standing high above the ground. Numerous people stood, strategically placed on a field of grass and dirt far below. White lines marked the field, comprising some kind of bounds where they positioned themselves. Hundreds of people watched the spectacle, cheering when one of the guys hit a ball with a stick. The others would try to catch it and tag the man before he could run in a large circle. If it reached one of the corners, he was safe, though that appeared to have its own set of rules.

Fenlara laughed. It seemed like an overly complicated game of fetch, though these people seemed to be enjoying themselves. But so did a dog running after its toy.

Stealing a glance at the spectators, Fenlara took a seat midway to the ground level. Her clothing shifted, adapting to her surroundings. She now wore a black hat with an 'M' and a picture of a fish on it. Her white shirt had black stripes along the hem and was slightly oversized. It had a name and number written on the back though she didn't bother reading what it said. A squishy glove shaped like an oversized hand with an extended finger rested on her left, while a sausage of some kind sat idle in a sliced roll in her right.

Now that she looked the part, she had to figure out exactly what it was they were all shouting about.

One of the men on the side of the field gave signal and a voice cut through the noise. "And the Marlin's call their last Time-Out. I'll tell ya, folks, this is gonna be a close game. With runners on second and third, these next few plays are pivotal. I can only imagine what's going through third baseman, Brian Anderson's head at this moment. He really has his work cut out for him."

Fenlara caught movement out the corner of her eye. She could feel the residual power lingering. Had she been anywhere else, she would have dismissed it. But not here. And not now.

Picking herself up, she approached the bricked wall. It was solid, yet the residue was unmistakable. Someone had opened the timestream here.

Locking onto the lingering energies, Fenlara carefully applied her own power and the doorway came open with ease. It was almost too easy, which meant her eyes hadn't deceived her. The vortex was only seconds fresh. That meant she had a time traveler on her hands.

Stepping through, Fenlara's armor and sword returned. She traveled through the timestream, floating in the swirling blue glow between everything. Despite the obvious movement, so quick she could hardly see the numerous events transpiring just beyond the ethereal walls, she felt like she was sitting still. Faster than time travel often left that impression. It was one of the first things she'd been taught. Trying to stop in the timestream was dangerous. If she caught any kind of drag, it could easily throw her through the wall and there was no telling where she'd end up.

Several moments passed before Fenlara felt her feet impact the ground. She wasn't entirely sure where she was, but it felt wrong. Once before she'd felt something like this. Only this was far worse. Every impulse told her to flee. It didn't matter where she was, she needed to leave and never look back. Not even dragon fear or demons commanded such strong impulse. That could only mean one thing. She was someplace forbidden to her.

Fenlara squared herself, adjusting to her new surroundings. Everything was cold and uninviting. Large rocks protruded, partially covered in thick layers of snow. A scent of sulfur lingered in the air. Becoming attuned with the energies, she felt the temporal power begin its flow. The crack in reality began to split, opening into the doorway she'd used so many times before.

A sudden impact rolled her eyes into the back of her head and her doorway disappeared. Fenlara crumbled to the rocky snow covered terrain, unconscious before she hit the ground.

The Duke Target

Levi Samuel

Chapter V

Temporal energy crackled around her, though it was not her own. Fenlara could feel it coursing throughout her body. Somehow her trip through the paradox had charged her with more power than she'd ever possessed. She was stronger than ever, though strength did little for pain. Time was the only remedy for that, the one commodity she was lacking.

Getting to her feet, Fenlara inspected her hands. Sparks jumped between her fingers, crackling each time she moved. It fueled her thoughts, challenging everything she knew. There was little doubt she could rebuild existence with a simple snap of her fingers, though that was a power reserved for the gods, a select few of them at that.

Reining herself in, Fenlara took a seat on her bed. It sprung a little with the sudden weight. She'd have to be careful holding this much power. It was intoxicating. The wrong thought could send her tumbling into the unknown. If only there was a way to dispose of it without risking everything around her.

Fenlara's eyes settled on the woman at her feet. For the briefest moment she'd forgotten all about their conundrum. It reinforced the danger she posed. If she could forget about someone so important to her, what could she do against someone she had no attachment to?

Sighing, Fenlara crawled from her bed and took position behind the woman. Time didn't move in this place like it did elsewhere. That would prolong her life. But she couldn't leave the wounds unattended either. The woman was safe here, albeit in immense amounts of pain. But for how long? A paradox was ripping apart the known world. If it came here, it likely already was, all it would take was a stray pocket of time and she could die in a moment's notice. Fortunately, the overcharge of power could help in that regard.

Staring intently at the blood-soaked clothing clinging to the lethal wound, Fenlara wondered how best to approached the situation. When she was a cleric it was nothing to rip the clothes away and inspect the wound before treatment. She didn't have that option here.

The woman's eyes stared blankly at the duke. She was numb, confused. All of this was foreign to her, though it made a lot more sense right before she was stabbed. She'd been abducted and tortured for something she hadn't done. At least not yet. Weak, unable to do anything but stare, she let the comfortable numb claim her.

Fenlara watched the woman's eyes close. Her already pale skin was chalky and white. Residue from sweat, blood, and tears clung to her flesh, having dried some time ago. It seemed she had nothing left to give. The duke smiled. Were they anywhere else she would have feared death, but that wasn't the case. Not yet. Death could not claim her here, not without time to carry her.

Studying the woman, Fenlara began to formulate a plan. The problem was, she couldn't risk touching her again, especially here. Doing so would guarantee both their deaths. It was their contact that had created the paradox they'd used to escape. To repeat the action would end this sanctuary and all it was connected to. There was no guarantee that wasn't already happening, but it made little sense to expedite the process.

Healing wounds was nothing new to her. She'd managed her fair share, both minor and severe. The problem she ran into was most healing magics required physical contact. How was she supposed to heal without touch? Moreover, how was she going to erase these memories if they managed to survive? That raised an even bigger question. Why did she not already remember? There was more at play here than she realized.

Focusing her will, Fenlara was pleased to feel much of the demon blood had passed. In fact, what little remained was being burned out by the excessive temporal power. That would open her up to the other dukes and Ozmodius, provided they were still alive.

Her focus came nearly on instinct. Tapping into her core, she bridged the gap between her magics. The raw energies began to boil, entwining themselves with her spell. Fenlara took a deep breath and exhaled slowly. She had to keep herself grounded, lest she'd fly off and do something foolish. That was what the magics wanted. They wanted to run wild and untamed. If she gave in, even for a second, there was no telling what she'd do. Nothing was beyond her limits, except maybe healing someone without touching them.

Her vision shifted, losing definition on the mundane around her. There wasn't much of it, especially here. Nearly everything began to glow, some things brighter than others. Detection of magic was a simple spell to most casters. It didn't answer more than a handful of questions. But to a Duke Tarset, it was a different spell entirely.

The connection to their god granted divine magics, but they were also skilled in the powers of the mind. Typically, these two magics were not interchangeable. In fact, most often they conflicted with one another. It took a master of both to combine them, but only a select few were capable of using one to fuel the other. Fenlara had questioned their marrying when it was taught to her, but there was no denying its broad range of benefits. When the temporal powers of a duke joined the mix, it opened an entirely new world of possibilities.

Gritting her teeth, forcing the chaotic combination to obey, Fenlara searched the woman before her. Nothing could remain hidden while using her pristine sight. Illusion magics were useless. Solids became transparent. Thermal energies displayed anywhere from bright red to dark blue. Magic burned bright, the intensity and color denoting type as well as strength. Time became meaningless, as did distance. She couldn't confirm it for lack of perception, but if she had to imagine what it felt like being a god, this particular spell was likely the answer.

It was the magic details Fenlara was searching for. She knew the energies within the hall, especially those of her room. She'd placed most of the items herself. But it was not her effects she was concerned with. She needed to know why she couldn't recall any of the events of the last few hours. More importantly, why this woman, and herself by extension, weren't already dead. The answers weren't with her, that meant the secrets had to lay with her ward.

Ignoring the clothing, Fenlara thoroughly inspected the body. She was a conglomeration of blue, gold, and white. The blue was unsettling as the body temperature was fading. There wasn't much she could do about it just yet. Even if she could touch her, the slightest healing spell could have dire consequences until she figured out why their link was fractured. Though perhaps not everything had to be magical in nature.

Lecturing herself, Fenlara pulled the blanket from her bed and draped it over the limp form. It wouldn't hinder her sight so long as her spell remained intact.

Seeing the blue lighten slightly, Fenlara moved on to the gold and white. She wasn't surprised by their presence. Her clerical abilities began to manifest in her early adolescents. By the time of the Demon Wars she'd developed the basics for what she soon learned to be psionics. It made sense this woman was the same. She was a younger entity of herself after all.

Fenlara paused a moment, wondering why they'd taken this version of her. This was her from the Demon Wars. She was a badass. Having mastered her skills as a cleric, she'd been sent as an ambassador to the front lines. It was there she learned of her psionic talents. Why go through all the trouble when abducting a child was so much easier to manage? There was only one answer that made sense.

Demon blood was both difficult to obtain and extremely dangerous to store, not to mention highly illegal to possess. About the only way to safely transport it was in the demon to whom it belonged. But the abyssal creatures weren't known for negotiating. Betrayal and deceit were bred in their nature, which made them suspicious of any kind of partnership. On occasion one would make a deal if they believed they had the upper hand. The dukes had played a pivotal role in their defeat during the first demon war. That made getting rid of them a high priority. And since the Pendulum was in the business of eliminating dukes, it stood to reason the exchange of demon blood was a reasonable trade. What better way than abducting a known thorn in their side who would eventually become a duke?

Fenlara shook her head, wiping the thought from her mind. She didn't have time to speculate right now. Surviving the ordeal had to be her first priority.

Studying the bruised and broken flesh, she felt remorse for everything that had happened. From the look of it, this woman, this younger form of herself, had been beaten and tortured far longer than she'd imagined. Fenlara as a duke had been in their custody no longer than a few hours, a day at most. From the age of these wounds, this girl, barely a woman, had been prisoner for at least a couple weeks. Many of the wounds had been trying to heal, though it was clear they'd been precisely reopened many times over.

The thought made her sick. They'd captured her younger self knowing who she was and who she'd become. They'd used that knowledge to lure her into a trap. All of this had been one sick plot to steal her powers and destroy her. But why didn't they just kill the younger one and be done with it? If they knew who she was, that was all it would take.

The question answered itself nearly as quick. The dukes were protected by the dukes. They couldn't visit their own timelines or the timelines of the people they knew in life. But other dukes, dukes from a different time could. If they'd gone after her without the lockout, they would have met resistance. As it were, she'd fallen into the trap. She'd caused the lockout by unwittingly entering her own timeline. That was why no other duke came. She'd accidently locked them out.

She was getting sidetracked. Forcing her attention to the task at hand, Fenlara plopped to her backside and shifted her vision to begin searching beneath flesh and meat. She should have seen something by now, but there were many layers to inspect. About halfway up her torso, a speck of energy came into view, disappearing just as quickly. "What was that?"

In all of time, past, present, or future, in all the places Fenlara had heard of or been, never had an energy of any kind escaped the pristine sight of a Duke Tarset. Why had this one? With renewed vigor, she sat up, moving as close as she dared.

The Pendulum knew to dose her with demon blood. And they'd made sure to trap her in a black zone. Was it out of the question to think they knew of her specific abilities as well?

Carefully, Fenlara pulled the blanket away and used her energies to lift the blood drenched robes. Having never thought to inspect her own powers with the sight spell, she was somewhat taken back by its appearance. A prismatic entity hovered over the body, clenched onto the ruined and tattered cloth. Its form was clearly ethereal and indefinite, but the multiple appendages reminded her of a spider. She wondered how her other abilities would look, though such an experiment would have to wait.

Locating the place where she'd seen the energy, Fenlara focused, forcing the flicker of power to show itself. It was subtle, little more than a spark hidden deep beneath the gold and white. Her eyes squinted and she leaned in to get a closer look. A small tattoo had been placed deep beneath the flesh on her ribs. If she had to guess it had been etched into bone.

Dropping her focus, Fenlara's sight returned to normal. Details began to clear and she found herself staring at the rended flesh and puckered scars. Seeing it as a whole, outside the prism of magic, she knew what she was looking at.

In a huff, the duke jumped to her feet and began digging beneath her armor. Both it and her tunic disappeared with a thought, leaving her bare for inspection. Twisting, searching her own ribs, Fenlara found the sigil marred beneath her right breast, though it had long since healed. "Damn them!"

The Duke Tarset

Levi Samuel

Chapter VI

"I don't understand." Fenlara watched the duke raise a slice of pizza overhead, catching the string of dripping cheese and topping in his mouth. Feeding it in, he took a large bite and began chewing.

"Unberstan wat?" Trendal asked through his overstuffed maw.

"We don't look like these people." She gestured to the patrons around them enjoying their various meals. Nobody paid them any mind other than what seemed to be an unintentional avoidance. People simply didn't look their way, or bother approaching the table in the middle of the room. Moreover, their clothing was of a style she'd never seen. There was so much color everywhere she looked. Some people wore long breeches in a variety of materials and thicknesses, others wore half pants. Some wore slim clinging dresses that barely covered any amount of flesh, while others wore partial hats that didn't appear to serve a purpose whatsoever. She didn't want to get started on the accessories. Carrying a coin purse or tobacco pipe was one thing, but these people had an assortment of odd devices they used without a second thought. Some covered their ears, held in place by thin straps that contorted around their heads. Smoked spectacles occasionally covered their eyes, though it didn't seem to matter whether they were inside or out, night or day, they wore them just the same.

"We're aspects of time. We don't belong here. It's for that reason most people aren't capable of perceiving us. It's the same reason they can't see magic. They don't accept anything outside their realm of understanding. They live in a society that breeds closed minds. It prevents them from experiencing anything beyond their realm of acceptance. Of course, exceptions can be made. A fireball to the face hurts just the same whether you believe in its existence or not." Trendal took another bite before laying the thick cheese, sauce, and meat covered bread back onto his plate.

"But we're wearing armor and carrying swords. Best I can tell, that practice is uncommon in this age. Surely, that warrants some attention? Look at that guy over there. He's big. Lots of muscle. I would have pegged him for a warrior from the start but for sitting here watching him." Fenlara shook her head. "He wouldn't know how to hold a sword, let alone swing one."

Trendal nodded his agreement. "Call it adaptive camouflage. We don't belong. We're fragments of reality slipping between the cracks. People don't want to see what they can't explain. They can't explain us, so their brains convince them we don't exist. As a result, they overlook us without realizing it." Trendal leaned against the back of his chair, scooting it from the table. "I'm thirsty. Do you want a drink?"

"Um, sure?"

The duke brought his hands in front of him, extending his thumbs and index fingers. One faced him, the other away, creating a rectangle between his appendages.

Fenlara could feel the energy build inside the little window but she couldn't yet tell what he was doing. Thus far, he'd done many things she didn't understand, though he always seemed happy to explain. Watching intently, a glossy film appeared and things began to move inside the window, contrast to their surroundings.

Trendal slowly pulled his hands apart, holding the form. The wider he pulled the larger the window became. A moment later he was staring through a hole into another time and place.

Keeping one hand stationary, he dropped the other and reached through. "Cream soda, root beer, strawberry?" He glanced to Fenlara, clearly lost in both his question and action.

"Um, I—don't care. The first one?" She shrugged for emphasis.

Retracting his hand, two glass bottles were locked between his fingers. One was full of a frosty bronze liquid while the other was red and bubbly. The window closed no sooner than his hand was clear. Setting the drinks on the table, he twisted the metal cap and laid it down, sliding the bottle to his companion.

Fenlara inspected the sleek container. Condensation was already forming on the outside of the glass. Inspecting the label, she didn't know what Jones Soda was, but apparently she was about to find out. Tipping the rim to her lips, she drank in the carbonated concoction, letting the flavor fill her senses. Setting it down, she swallowed and a big smile formed upon her lips.

"Pretty good, huh?" A knowing smirk was ever present on the duke. "What's the fun in navigating time if you can't enjoy the luxuries from every age?"

"You'd know more than I. Now, back to this camouflage thingy. You're telling me they can't see or hear us simply because they don't believe we exist? What happens when we have to interact with them? And what about the guy with the gun? He seemed to be able to see us."

"Ah!" Trendal took another swig and set his strawberry soda in front of him. "The guy last night could not see us. He would have robbed those people whether we were there or not. The boy was an abnormality. Had his parents died he would have gone into a spiral of self-loathing and vigilante justice which would have eventually ended with him entering our realm of expertise. By saving his parents, we stopped a whole mess of problems before they could start. We just used the robber for training purposes. He has no memory or recollection of us whatsoever. As for your other point. Yes, we occasionally have to interact with them, but that's a little more complex."

"How so?"

"Temporal magics aren't always cooperative. They can alter your timestream in the most unexpected ways. Even now we're being affected by it. The longer we stay here, the stronger the pull will become. If we overstay our welcome we can become the abnormality which we're sworn to repair. Additionally, if the abnormality is a living person, they don't belong here either, which means they can see us without looking. That can cause some problems for someone who doesn't realize there's more to the world than what they've been taught. For that you need to blend in."

"That makes sense, but how? It's not like I brought my pack with a change of clothes. And you've made it pretty clear that magic isn't always reliable."

"That all depends on where and when you are." Trendal lifted a golden pocket watch from nowhere. Opening the case, he inspected inside and closed it once again. It was gone before his hand fell. "We're running out of time until our next job so I'll make this quick." He stood and straightened his robes.

Fenlara hadn't noticed until this moment that his armor was gone.

"Magic is extremely rare in this age but it still exists. That's a whole other long story that we don't have time for at the moment, but that particular detail is important to this scenario. Let's say we need to speak with that guy over there."

Trendal pointed to a man who had most of his head shaven and polished to a glossy shine. Only a single row of black perfectly shaped spikes ran the center of his head. He wore a denim jacket minus the sleeves, which revealed a black tee shirt beneath. And there was enough metal in his face to forge a sword.

Fenlara studied the man for a moment. She was surprised she knew the names for such attire, but Trendal told her she would. Temporal knowledge, he'd called it. Names, places, and actions, as well as any important events of the age would passively soak into her mind. It was another duke ability. Exposure would ensure she knew common knowledge of each era she visited. It was for this reason she knew that the man to whom Trendal was referring belonged to the *Punk* crowd, and that they were in a time called the *eighties*. Prior to this exact moment, she hadn't known either of those two details.

"If I needed to interact with him, the adaptive magics would do one of two things. Either I'd be completely hidden from his perception, unable to be heard, seen, felt, or any other sense that could denote my presence. I'd be little more than a ghost haunting him. Or I could be perceived as someone he can relate to. My armor and robes would fade away, leaving me clothed in whatever persona his mind could accept. I would have no choice in the matter regardless of which path occurred. Now, let's say for the sake of argument that my interaction with him is completely necessary and too important to leave to chance. I can't have him influencing how he perceives me, but I also can't approach him dressed like someone out of a cheesy fantasy novel. In that instance, I can simply will my appearance to become whatever I desire." The dark robes and sword faded away. In their stead a pair of torn blue jeans and a gray tee shirt with the sleeves ripped off appeared. The duke's long red hair began to darken and pull itself into a spikey pose. Dark eyeliner encircled his eyes, and in a heartbeat he no longer looked anything like the man he was moments before. In fact, the only link to his former appearance was a small necklace in the shape of a metal hourglass that dangled over his sternum.

"I see. So what happens if you need your sword, or if something hits you unaware? Aren't you going to want your armor?" Fenlara was genuinely curious. She'd absorbed so much information in such a short time, but it was all so new and exciting. Not even the Demon Wars could have prepared her for such a change in perspective.

"That's the beauty of the augmentation. My armor is still here. As is my sword. Though neither are often needed. But when they are, they're always present." He gave a gentle knock over his chest, allowing the unique unseen metal to ring out. "Now, if you'll excuse me a moment, I have some work to do."

Fenlara watched the duke approach the punk man. She couldn't hear what was being said as they spoke just over a whisper, but they greeted each other as brothers.

The man nodded excessively and balled his fist. Bringing it near his face, he shook it in some kind of silent cheer, got up and left.

Trendal returned to the table, took another bite of pizza, downed the remainder of his soda, and nodded for Fenlara to follow.

Chapter VII

"Do you realize how stupid this is?"

"Shut it! The boss gave his orders. How we follow them is up to us."

"Come on, Damion. She's a duke. You're messing with things beyond your understanding."

The voices broke through the silence and void. A pain throbbed in the back of Fenlara's head, but it was more than a simple headache. She'd been hit. That much was clear, but it was the strange taste in her mouth that demanded answers. Her body ached all over, like she'd been beaten to a pulp and the bruises had yet to heal.

"Shut your mouth, she's waking."

Fenlara listened to the approaching footsteps, though she couldn't see to whom they belonged. The air was crisp and stagnant, smelling strongly of sulfur and smoke. A mild warmth radiated somewhere to her right, insufficient for the space provided. She could hear tree limbs clapping in a heavy breeze, though none of it reached her. That meant she was inside some kind of shelter, but more information was needed.

The cold and soggy earth soaked into her breeches. The moist fabric was heavy, clinging to her backside and legs. Judging from what felt like trampled grass or possibly moss beneath her, she was on an open floor. That left the options of a tent or a cave, though the lack of echo and excessive cold ruled out the latter.

Struggling to move, Fenlara realized she'd been lashed to something solid. It snagged on the fibers of her sleeves and had the feel of rough-cut wood. This had to be one of the support posts.

Whoever these men were, they'd made a mistake. She hadn't become a duke by happenstance. Her skill in magics had taken her far, long before she'd accepted her calling.

Summoning the powers within her, Fenlara focused on her surroundings. Just because she was hooded and bound didn't mean she was helpless. One of her abilities was capable of melting iron to slag or crippling everyone in the area with little more than a high tone. All it took was a mere thought and steady concentration.

To her surprise, neither took effect, nor did any of the other tricks she had up her sleeve. All that resulted was a mind splitting headache that forced her to abandon the attempt.

A soft chuckle echoed in the darkness, directly to her left. "Struggle all ya want, girly. Ya ain't going nowhere."

The hood was ripped away, the coarse fabric scraping her ears as it passed. Blinding light filled her vision, having grown accustomed to the dark. It took a long moment for the spots to fade but Fenlara found herself as she'd expected, lashed to a post in the middle of a large tent. There was a small wood stove near the wall to the right. A hole in the ceiling allowed the flue to escape, providing the only source of light the room had to offer. Now that her eyes were adjusting, it was less bright than she'd initially thought. A few lanterns hung here and there on iron hooks, but they weren't lit. Turning her attention to the men, Fenlara felt a hatred burn inside her. They knew what they were doing. And for that, they would pay.

Fenlara attempted to speak. She wanted to scream her rage and demand they release her. She was a Duke Tarset, a cleric of Ozmodius before that. Surely that would make them see reason. As it were, not a sound escaped her. She didn't have to be a master of magics to know a silence spell when she encountered one.

The towering man smiled cheerfully, displaying a single golden tooth among a mouthful of neglected yellow ones. "Ya didn't expect me to let ya run amok did ya? I can't have ya throwing powerful words and the like all over the place. That's a good way to get dead." Contorting his smile into a sadistic frown, his nose wrinkled as he shook his head. "Nah, ya didn't think that. Ya're a duke. I hear yer kind is smarter than that."

"Damion, enough. Let's just do the job and be done with it." The man near the door pleaded. He was much younger and cleaner by appearance. If anything, he didn't fit the bill of a maniacal bad guy but looks could be deceiving.

Damion glared over his shoulder at his younger counterpart. "This the last time I'm gonna tell ya boy, shut up! This ain't my first rodeo. Maybe once ya've dealt with half as many dukes, I'll take yer advice. Now, make yourself useful and grab me one of those canisters from the box in there." He gestured to the next room over.

The younger man disappeared around the corner.

This wasn't his first duke? Fenlara repeated to herself. *How many had fallen to these men? More importantly, what were they hoping to achieve?* She could hear the younger of the two shuffling around in the next room, though he was of little concern. It was Damion she had to be weary of. He had a look she'd seen a few times during her travels. This man enjoyed causing pain. He liked hurting people. For him, it was more than a job. It was entertainment. Gritting her teeth, she tried to fight past the pain and find her focus. If she could manage that, nothing could hold her. But how could she fight it? The more she tried, the worse it hurt.

"I can see what ya're doing. I'm afraid it ain't gonna work. Ya see, I've got this little cocktail that keeps people like ya nice and complacent." He pulled a transparent bag that had been hanging on the post into view.

Fenlara stared intently at the dark bubbling liquid within. She could feel the evil radiating inside. That's what was causing her headache. But worse, how did these men get ahold of it? Something so wrong was forbidden across all the realms. Not to mention they'd been sealed long before—the thought told her exactly where she was. Moreover, it told her why she was so desperate to leave. Her fears renewed with the possibilities of what her presence here could represent.

"I see ya know what this is. And now ya know why yer prayers ain't being answered. Yer little god doesn't want ya now that ya're full of demon blood."

The younger man reappeared holding a cylindrical device not much wider than a balled fist and about as long as his forearm. A mesh could be seen behind the glass windows that wrapped the sides. Across the top a round cap had been engraved with numerous sigils.

"Took ya long enough." Damion mocked, ripping the canister from the younger man's hands. He twisted the cap, aligning the sigils and pulled the innards free.

The mesh began to glow a deep purple and Fenlara felt the siphon latch onto her. She'd never seen a temporal battery in person, but she knew what it was. Trendal had described them when he was training her. The dukes occasionally used them to store excess temporal energy or to calm an unstable timestream. They'd only been used a handful of times, and only under the direst circumstances. So much power had a tendency to corrupt, which had made them a tool of last resort.

It seemed these men not only found a stash of them, but learned to use it as a weapon. What did that mean for her?

Fenlara struggled to find an answer. Nothing favorable came to mind. If they drained her power, especially here, all of existence was likely to crumble in the wake of her demise. Was that intentional? Or were they simply messing with powers they didn't understand? Either way they had to be stopped.

The Duke Target

Levi Samuel

Chapter VIII

Most would never have known what the demonic sigil meant. As it were, she was one of the few who did. The Demon Wars were a time of great struggle for the people of Ur. Fenlara had been fortunate enough to miss the first installment. By the end of it, the realm had been sundered and overrun by the foul creatures. And while the free peoples of the realm won in the end, it was not without great costs.

The air had become toxic and the ground was no longer able to yield crops. As a result, the old world was abandoned. Scores of people flocked to the Eldar cities. It was there the alliance of free people entered the new world, sealing the old one behind them. But peace rarely last long. Eventually, the demons found the new world and began a new conquest to finish what they'd started.

Fenlara's grandfather had been one of the thousands to make the initial trek through the portal so long ago. When the demons returned, he'd long perished. But the time for old heroes was over. The church of Ozmodius was known throughout the lands. People came from near and far to pray or ask blessing. One such blessing, though she didn't think so at the time, was Fenlara being assigned to accompany a group of adventurers into the wild. Until then she'd only known life within the blackened halls of the Temple of Winstead.

During her travels many of the demons had begun taking prisoners. They'd chain them into their crude gateways, using their lifeforce to summon more of their kind. The realm was sealed after all. The only way through was with powerful magics. But the prisoners were only good for a single use and due to the efforts of Fenlara and her group, many of those attempts were cut short.

After many setbacks, the demons began to evolve. Rather than throwing their limited forces at the problem as they had so many times in the past, they began to think efficiently. Their dwindling numbers meant less captives. And less captives meant they couldn't summon reinforcements. The prizes became smaller, less noticeable, and over time the threat all but disappeared. At least that's what most believed at the time.

In secret, having amassed thousands of prisoners in their exodus, the demons resurfaced in force. They'd found a way to forcefully preserve life, keeping their prisoners alive for continuous torment and use. And it was all due to a demonic sigil that had been carved into their flesh. Starvation, mutilation, even complete evisceration could not free them from their bonds so long as the mark remained. Fenlara now had an extremely similar mark buried beneath her skin.

Recalling her efforts during the last Demon War, memory of the prison camps came flooding back. The dark energies left their victims twisted and broken. Her magics had been all but useless in healing them. In fact, most of the time the effect was opposite. Fenlara would never forget the first time she tried. Her magics took hold, only their intention had been inverted. Instead of healing, she was forced to listen to the agonizing screams until they fell silent. She could still see the blood boiling, cooking through flesh and rotten meat. Of the thousands they'd freed from those camps, less than twenty people survived.

Still, the effects of that sigil were somewhat different than hers. If the mark was preventing death, why did Damion believe he could kill her? Surely he knew what he was doing. Everything else had been planned to the finest detail. Even when she took his life his confidence never wavered. Was this another piece of the puzzle she had yet to figure out?

Fenlara picked herself up and began pacing the room. Her tunic and armor returned. There were so many questions racing through her mind. It reminded her of Trendal's second rule of combat. She had to anticipate her opponent. Once she got ahead, she could strike. But how was she to get ahead of this? There were too many unknown variables.

How could they have anticipated she'd create the paradox and escape? It was a huge risk. Paradoxical energies were chaotic at best. Once such a wild element was introduced nothing could be guaranteed. But what if guarantee wasn't the intention? What if the paradox itself had been their goal? Why else would they put her in the same room with her younger self? Once the raw energies were unleashed, what happened to her was of little concern. And with her death being currently impossible, it wouldn't take anything to be eternally lost inside a paradox. But the question remained. How could they have planned all of that?

It was times such as these Fenlara wished she could witness her own future. It would relieve so much uncertainty. She paused, repeating the statement to herself. Why couldn't she? The timeline was already broken. Any possible future she could witness would be an abstract of what was supposed to be. And with her overcharge of paradox energy, surely such a feat was within her capabilities.

Unleashing the energies crackling around her, Fenlara brought her hands together, fingers and thumbs extended. Pulling the window open, she searched what was left of existence, hoping to find anything to help her. If only the prize was so delicious as a frosty Jones Soda.

The Duke Tarset

Levi Samuel

Chapter IX

Colors swished by, blended together in streaks of swirling light. Fenlara had no clue where they were going, and Trendal didn't appear to have any intention of telling her. Occasionally, she'd catch a glimpse of something solid, a building, some strange creature, or a crowd of people, but the vision was gone before she could gather any details. In fact, the only constant to all of this was an instinct that told her she was getting closer to their destination. It reminded her of her time in the monastery as a child.

There wasn't much to do for fun when your life consisted of study, lecture, and mass. That left the children to find their own means of entertainment. One of the many games they played required her to be blindfolded. She'd stumble around the place, trying to avoid anything breakable while the other kids would shout out hotter or colder.

If the same rules applied, she was burning hot, though the timestream was much harder to see through than a scrap of cloth.

Finally, existence came into view and Fenlara felt her feet impact the ground. It was a subtle impact, like transitioning from a set of stairs to the floor, but noticeable nonetheless. "Where are we?"

"Can't you feel it?" Trendal asked, glancing back at her as he continued to walk.

It was a simple time, similar to what she'd grown up with. One thing was certain, she wouldn't have trouble blending in. "It feels like when I was a child, though older. Like before I was born."

A soft chuckle escaped the elder duke. "You're not wrong. But I want you to explore those feelings a little deeper. See if you can figure it out before we arrive."

Taking a deep breath, Fenlara followed in silence, attempting to locate whatever it was he wanted her to find. She could still feel the hot-cold tracker, which was screaming she was right on top of whatever it was. She wasn't in physical pain, but it was certainly an uncomfortable feeling. Whatever was happening here, she didn't want to be so close to it. It was something that should happen without her presence. "I feel like I shouldn't be here."

"That's it." Trendal approached one of the crude hovels and opened the door.

Inside was dimly lit. Candlelight flickered off the walls, dancing in the breeze from the doorway. Somewhere inside, a woman moaned out. A deep male voice followed, offering comfort.

Stepping through the opening, Trendal paused, setting his focus on the younger duke. "Whatever you do, don't touch anything unless I tell you to."

Fenlara nodded and followed him inside.

Once the door was closed, the light became more intense. The crackle of a burning hearth could be heard amidst the crying moans.

The pair of dukes rounded the corner to find a handful of people surrounding a wood framed bed. The mattress was dirty and stained. The seams had burst in many spots, spilling straw onto the floor. The décor was simple. Pots hung from hooks in the wooden walls. A broom leaned in the corner. And a small table was piled with dishes and what appeared to be a few loafs of stale bread.

Fenlara inspected the place thoroughly, uncertain what it was that made her want to flee. For an old farmhouse this place was thoroughly rundown.

Of the two men, the one kneeling beside the bed glanced at the pair of dukes and got to his feet. "Ah, I'm pleased you made it. I feared the church hadn't received my message in time." He reached out, taking Trendal's hand into his thick meaty paws. Shaking vigorously, he smiled as if they were his saviors returned after a long absence.

The other man, who'd been standing on the far side of the bed came around and approached. "I've done all I can for her. My herbs aren't helping. If we don't get this baby out soon, neither of them will last the night. Is there anything you can do?"

Trendal looked from the two men to the woman in labor and the midwife beside her. "I'll do what I can, though I need a few things."

"Anything!" The stout man proclaimed, releasing his grip.

"First, I need everyone to clear the room. My assistant here will notify you when it's safe to return. I'll also need a pot of boiling water, and a handful of roseweed if you've got some on hand."

"Aye, Julieta, get the water."

"I've got some roseweed in my shop." The botanists added.

"Thank you, Gerdan."

The three spectators cleared out, leaving the two dukes alone with the pregnant woman.

Approaching the bed, Trendal stared down at her, noting the sweat clinging to her skin. Carefully, he placed the back of his hand upon her forehead. "Fenlara, toss another log and stoke the fire. We need to bring the temperature up."

Fenlara went to work as commanded. She wasn't sure what any of this had to do with her, though the longer she stayed the stronger her desire to leave became.

Suddenly, the panting moans ceased. The flames halted their licking, and the sparks held in midair.

Fenlara looked around, surprised by the unexpected timestop. Getting to her feet, she approached Trendal. To her surprise, he was just as still as the flames she'd left. *What could be so powerful as to freeze him?*

Amidst the calm and quiet, wailing cries echoed.

Fenlara looked down to see the head of a baby enter the world. It was covered in a thick glossy film. Blood and slime clung to its exposed dark hair and red skin. "Um, Trendal!" She wasn't sure what to do. Why had time stopped? And why was this baby not frozen like everyone else? More importantly, she'd been told not to touch anything. She was a cleric and had been present at the delivery of a few babies, but she'd never done it herself. What if her interaction with this child had some unforeseen consequences? "Trendal!" Fenlara placed her hand on the duke's arm, giving him a solid shake.

The moment her hand altered him, Trendal awoke. "I understand now." He announced to no one in particular.

"Understand what? What's happening?"

"This child is unique. More so than I originally thought."

"No shit! What's happening?"

He smiled and waved his hand, dismissing her question. "I have to remove the timestop before the child runs out of air." Contorting his fingers, Trendal brought his hands together in an audible clap. The woman's cries returned and the flames began to lap again.

It took no time at all for the birthing process to conclude. Fenlara stared at the baby, wrapped in a blanket and placed in her mother's arms. She wanted to hold it. She'd been present at its birth after all. But a stronger part of her wanted nothing to do with it. There was something about the child that didn't agree with her. Something far stronger than the power clearly within it.

"Fenlara, would you gather the others and wait for me outside?"

She nodded, unable to find any words worth speaking. Reaching the door, Fenlara stepped out to find the father waiting a short distance away. He was huddled over a small fire, watching a pot that refused to boil. The midwife waited beside him, wrapped in a quilted blanket. "You can go in now."

They looked up in unison and made for the door. "What is it?" The man asked, pushing his way through the narrow opening.

"A girl." Fenlara stepped aside to keep from being trampled. Once the door was closed, she approached the fire and took a seat where the midwife had been. It was a cool night, though not overly cold. Even if it were, temperature didn't affect dukes like it did most people. They were masters of magic. Finding comfort in almost any environment was little more than a parlor trick for them.

Trendal stepped through the door after a long while. He looked exhausted and sweat was clearly running down his face. It was an odd sight for someone such as him, though to a normal human it wouldn't have been anything out of the ordinary. But he was far from ordinary.

"What the hell happened in there?" Fenlara asked, finding no pleasure in the question. Something about this entire thing was wrong, though exactly what continued to elude her.

Trendal took a deep breath before speaking. Steam rose from him, disappearing into the night sky. "We just witnessed the birth of a crucible."

"What's that? And why—how did its timestop work on you but not me?"

"Many of the answers I could give you would be speculation only. In truth, I don't know why it influenced me. That's never happened before. I can say your ancestors were in that room. That's why I told you not to touch anything. I couldn't have you accidently doing anything to change your history. We're on the edge of your timeline, which is why you don't feel comfortable here. I wanted you to know what it felt like so you can identify it at a later date. As for the crucible, it's hard to say what it will become. Think of it as a host. It's a living body, aging and growing the way any normal person would, but in a sense, it's hollow. An empty vessel so to speak. One day something or someone may need it. When that day comes, they'll take residence in it."

"Who would do such a thing?"

"Gods usually. They can't walk the mortal plane outside a physical body. That leaves them with the option of sharing with a mortal or creating an empty vessel for use at a later time. Most of the gods I've met aren't overly good at sharing."

"What'll happen to her?"

"Hard to say. She may live her entire life and never be called to service. Or it could happen tomorrow. The only thing that's certain, all crucibles have command of great powers. It's a defense against an untimely demise. That's why she was able to create a timestop. Perhaps she perceived me as a threat, and you as a savior. But like I said, that's all speculation."

"All right. Can we get out of here? I don't like this place."

Chapter X

It was an odd feeling, having the power ripped from her. It began as a small tingle in the pit of her stomach, like a numbness that set in after heavy exhilaration. It didn't hurt, at least not at first. Over time it became more intense, absorbing more than just the temporal magics. That's how it felt anyway. It was like her soul was being forcefully torn apart and pulled from her. In truth she couldn't be sure exactly what it was doing but it wasn't a pleasant experience.

The siphon worked fast and efficient. Her energy levels had already dropped substantially and she'd only been exposed to it for a few minutes.

Sweat beaded upon Fenlara's brow. Her eye lids grew heavy, threatening to close. It took every ounce of effort to remain conscious. Panting heavily, Fenlara slouched, her movement restrained by the binds. Had they not been so tight, there was no doubt she would have toppled over.

Her strength waning rapidly, all she could do was try to remain conscious until she found an opportunity to break free. That was the only fortunate side to all of this. The more her strength faded, the more brazen her captors became. In their minds they'd already won.

That was the light at the end of this tunnel. All that was stopping her was the demon blood. If there was some way to flush it out, or prevent any more from entering, maybe she'd be able to do something—anything more than wait for them to kill her. But how could she manage that without use of her abilities? It wasn't as if she could slip the ropes.

Realizing she'd closed her eyes once again, Fenlara shook her head in a desperate attempt to wake. She wasn't sure how much longer she could hold out. Whoever these men were, they knew what they were doing, though it remained unclear as to why.

"I think she's had enough." The younger of the two pleaded, watching from the edge of the partition.

"I'll tell ya when she's had enough! I didn't come all this way just to fill a battery."

"Look at her, man. How much more can you get? Just put her out of her misery and be done with it."

"I'm gonna take as much as I can. And when she's empty and it starts draining her lifeforce, I'm gonna take some more. Ya ain't dealt with these assholes like I have. Ya think she'd show either of us any mercy if she got half the chance? No, she'd see the both of us utterly destroyed just for daring to cross her. They gotta learn they ain't the baddest dogs in the yard no more!"

Fenlara watched the pair from the corner of her eye. That was all she could manage. Even in her current state, she could feel the conflict waging within the younger man. He didn't enjoy what he'd become a part of. Even when he begged for her death, it wasn't out of malice or desire. He was asking for mercy. She didn't have a lot, but perhaps there was something more to him, something that could help her.

Watching the young man for as long as she dared, Fenlara studied him. There was a familiarity in his appearance, but the connection remained beyond her reach. He'd been the voice of reason on more than one occasion thus far, yet the other one clearly had seniority. That, paired with the conversation she'd overheard when they believed her unconscious, meant this was all part of something bigger. That raised a greater concern. Who was this *Master* they spoke of, and how was it he had access to temporal batteries?

Reaching Purgatory wasn't an overly difficult feat for any skilled traveler. She'd visited herself a time or two during the Demon Wars. But to get to the supply room within the Hall of Guardians? That was a feat unheard of. Never before had anyone entered the hall without permission, until now it seemed.

Fenlara chased the rabbit, compiling a list of possible suspects. The most protected rooms required a mirror walker, or something that allowed the talent. Only a handful of those existed. Of course, all of it was pointless to speculate. These people were in the business of draining dukes. Who was to say they weren't using the stolen magics to access the hall?

A crack echoed inside her and Fenlara felt the pain increase tenfold. She winced, tensing her muscles against the unseen attack but it was hopeless. Nothing could aid what was happening inside her.

She heard a clap across the room and Damion let out a delighted chuckle.

"Looks like we just reached the good stuff!" He slapped the younger man on the shoulder, nearly knocking him over.

Straining against the growing agony, Fenlara turned away from the two men and lifted her head to see the battery. It rested atop a small table a few feet away. The glowing mesh had been a vibrant purple when they started. Now it was growing darker, turning more of a deep red. She didn't know what that meant, but from the feel of it, it wasn't good.

A violent spasm shot through her and she felt her stomach wrench. Bile and blood worked its way up her throat, expelling down the front of her an into her lap. She wondered if it would have been less painful had she eaten. When she'd been sick, prior to her cleric days, it always seemed to hurt less when her stomach wasn't empty. As it were, dukes didn't have to eat as frequently as normal people, but their bodies still had to be maintained. The same applied to sleep. It wasn't often, about once every few weeks seemed to do the trick. In her current predicament, she wished she'd partaken a little more of both.

Groaning, she let the ropes take her weight and her eyes closed. She'd certainly feel better after a short nap. What could be the harm in that?

No! Fenlara demanded aloud, though the sound remained absent. *I have to keep fighting!* Shaking herself, she sat upright once again. There had to be a way out of this.

Each heartbeat renewed the intense throbbing inside her head, though it had slowed drastically in her weakened state. Perhaps that was the key? If she slowed her heart, the demon blood couldn't pump as fast. Maybe that would give her enough room to break free. But how long would it take?

Exploring her mental confines, she poked at the walls, searching for any weak spots. Everything was sealed tight, though there was one area that had a little give. She pushed against it, forcing her will. It held tight, though it wasn't nearly as strong as it had been. Pushing again, she felt a pop and a small window opened.

She paused, giving her mind a break. Her efforts were limited after all. She didn't want to strain too much until she could make some real progress. Though the question she had to ask herself was why had she not found it sooner? Maybe it was the fact that she'd gone nearly dormant, or maybe it was Ozmodius trying to help her. She couldn't say. Though she wasn't going to waste any opportunity that presented itself.

Taking a few deep breaths, preparing herself for what was to come, Fenlara locked onto the window and forced every bit of willpower she had into it. She abandoned every other thought and desire. Nothing mattered but this one solitary task. Her body trembled and her pulse raised. The vicelike grip of the demon blood was growing strong once again. A war drum echoed inside her head, demanding she abandon the fight. It whispered, promising every desire if she'd just give in. It assured her surrender was the only option. She'd be set free if she would only stop fighting. Freedom was guaranteed. She'd be free of pain, free of torture, free of life. She just had to lay down her metaphorical sword.

Fenlara screamed, thankful for the first time that she was silenced. She couldn't take much more. It clouded her mind, blocking her focus. Gritting her teeth, squeezing her fist as hard as she could, her body shook violently, thrashing against the bonds. Blood seeped from her ears. Her usual pale skin turned a deep red. Throbbing at her core, squeezing the slightest thought from her mind, Fenlara broke through.

"Damion, she's dying!" The younger man jumped up and rushed to her.

Fenlara could barely see him through blurred vision. She'd made it through. She was free. Before the first thought could occur to her, dizziness took hold. Her world began to spin, and everything went dark.

The Duke Tarset

Levi Samuel

Chapter XI

A rumbling quake shook the Hall of Guardians. Fenlara could hear the roar beyond the clock covered walls. She'd been correct in assuming the paradox was still present, not that there was any question. It merely confirmed her theory while announcing the time. If it was so close, that could only mean much of creation had been unmade. Once the raw energies tore through the hall, all of existence would be washed away like a sandcastle in a tide. There would be no hope for repair. There would be no one left to repair it.

Her attention returned to the limp form beside her. Fenlara felt sorry for the girl—herself. Neither of them had started this, but they'd played a pivotal role in it. It was up to them to stop it before it was too late.

The weight of existence was much heavier than she'd imagined, but it settled on her shoulders. No one else was available to share the load.

Fenlara stared through the window she'd created moments earlier. It wasn't nearly as comforting as the glass panes she'd looked out so many times throughout her youth. She'd always taken joy in the sights. Sunshine would cascade across the green leaves and grass. Trees would dance in a gentle breeze, while squirrels frolicked and chased each other around the thick trunks. Birds pecked at the ground and carried worms to their hatchlings. It was all so pleasant and simple. That wasn't the case any longer. Through this window all she could see was death and destruction. Storms ravaged the land, wiping away entire continents in the blink of an eye. People were swept away from their families, never to be reunited. Entire land masses and points in time were eradicated like dust in the wind.

Tears rolled down her cheeks. She'd created this mess. She'd been responsible for all this destruction. It was her fault. She'd been a pawn, sure. But she created the paradox. She'd failed to see the game until it was too late. Had she taken any other course of action, all of this could have been avoided.

Fenlara sniffed, wiping away the tears. Blaming herself was counterproductive. She had to do what no one else could. She had to fix something otherwise unfixable. But how? Even if she could find and stop whoever was behind it, how was she to undo a paradox. They were raw untamed energy. How was she to compete with something so vast and powerful?

One time point disappeared after another, leaving a static haze to fill the screen. She scanned the channels, flipping from one to another, searching for anything. She had the entertainment age to thank for the idea. She'd spent the better part of a day watching what was called *Television*. It hadn't been a productive use of her time, but she'd enjoyed it. If nothing else, it taught her how people of that age spoke. Though none of it would matter if she couldn't find what she was looking for. She wasn't even sure what that was.

Only a few places remained, and none of them were untouched. Fenlara watched the dark clouds swirling through, swallowing everything in their path. Soon there would be nothing left, and once it was all gone, she'd be the last to perish. Not even the gods were likely to survive. Even if they did, they'd simply rebuild somewhere else. Why waste time on something so corrupt as the mortal plane?

A loud crash echoed, knocking several of the clocks from the wall. Springs exploded and glass shattered, flying in all directions. A swirling vortex of gray and blue, riddled with lightning, cut through the cracks of stone and mortar. Debris and broken timepieces hit the ground just long enough to be sucked out.

The forceful winds pulled at her. Bracing herself, Fenlara fought against the vacuum. If either her doppelganger or herself were swept away everything would be lost.

Releasing her hold on the window, the duke was surprised to see it didn't disappear. She wondered if it was due to the excess powers inside her, or if the vortex was feeding it. It didn't matter either way. She had more important matters to attend.

Throwing her back against the side of the desk, Fenlara lifted and pushed the wooden device against the wall. The flat top sucked tight, buying her a few moments. That gave her an idea.

Rushing to her bed, Fenlara tore the mattress away and used it to block another crack. In moments the largest gaps were covered and the pressure began to ease.

Her back against the bottom of the box spring, Fenlara stared blankly at the walls. It was this moment she realized just how bare they were. Only a few clocks remained, less than twenty by her count. If each one lorded over a fixed point in time, there wasn't much of anything left.

Sounds echoed around her. The roar of the paradox, the cries of the dead with no one to usher them to the abyss, voices on the edge of eternity. Among all of it, a single tone managed to cut through the rumble and roar. She couldn't hear what was being said but whatever it was, it was commanding.

Returning to her window, Fenlara found one image within reach. She couldn't tell when, or even where the scene was. The paradox had swept across, mixing the remaining times into one last point of existence. The worlds were blended. A castle perched in the mountains, overlooking a huge metropolitan. Men and elves and orcs littered the streets. Cars and horses and wagons were crashed and mangled. And all of it was wrong.

Staring intently at the scene before her, Fenlara noticed a man standing upon the edge of a bluff, overlooking the chaos. His arms were raised overhead. His cloak and hair whipped in the heavy wind. He shouted into the heavens, demanding it obey his command. And to her surprise, it seemed to sooth the destruction.

Fenlara watched him intently. She couldn't see who he was, but there was no mistaking the armor. In the last place of time, in the direst of circumstances, against all odds, she'd managed to find another duke.

Another section of wall gave way, dislodging the desk. It tumbled into the violent forces swirling just outside her room. The force pulled at her arms, pulled at her body, dragging her toward oblivion. Her boots slid against the hard floor, unable to find traction. There was nothing to grab hold of. Everything was already gone. Helpless to stop it, Fenlara glanced at her unconscious counterpart lying beneath the overturned bed.

The swirling storm was so strong, so forceful. Fenlara reached for the hole in the wall, her fingers digging for anything they could find. It was too late. She was gone, floating helplessly into the chaos.

Chapter XII

Fenlara awoke to the warmth of a hand upon her cheek. Groggily, her vision returned and she found herself staring up at the younger of her two captors. There was a compassion in his eyes she hadn't expected to see. What's more, the heat of his touch lingered long after his hand had fallen. It reminded her of healing magic, though surely it was just wishful thinking. In her current state, she'd imagine nearly anything if it could help her. Though there was no denying the throbbing headache had lessened significantly.

Damion kicked the younger man, knocking him over. "Get away from her and go get me something to drink!" His vicious glare locked onto the duke, challenging her to try anything.

Fenlara watched the younger man pick himself up and rush for the entrance.

He paused just inside, staring back at her as if to apologize. Meeting her gaze, he turned away and ducked outside.

Her attention shifted to the vicious man towering over her. Returning her own defiant glare, she wondered what had happened to him to warrant such hatred. Whatever it was, it was likely deserved. The dukes didn't go around messing with people for no reason.

"Ya see what happens when ya fight?" Damion asked, smiling his victory. He leaned toward her, stopping inches from her face. "The demon blood keeps ya compliant. It keeps ya in your place." He squeezed the bag hanging above her, forcing more of the demonic fluid into the tube.

If ever there was a time she wished for progress, it was now. The stench of his breath made her want to gag. Turning her head away as best she could, Fenlara pulled herself upright to remove the pressure from her ribs. She was amazed by how much she could feel through the armor, though it was never an ordinary breastplate. Maybe it was her waning powers, or perhaps subconsciously she believed she'd be more comfortable in something a little less ridged. Whatever the case, her bindings weren't nearly so taut now that the armor had softened. It wasn't much but it gave her a little wiggle room.

"I'm glad ya've still got some fight left. Maybe ya'll fill the battery before it drains yer life away." Smiling his victory, Damion stood and approached the siphon. Twisting the dial at the top, the glow intensified, turning from its deep red to a near black.

Wincing in pain, Fenlara's teeth mashed in a desperate attempt to withstand the draw. It felt as if her insides were being liquified and pulled through her skin. Only once had she felt anything similar.

A demon warlord had attracted the attention of her group. During their battle, he'd unleashed some kind of channeled spell that sucked the life out of everyone in the area. She'd been a little too close when it hit, but they'd managed to land the killing blow before it finished her. As painful as that encounter had been, it was nothing compared to the pain she felt now.

"I bet ya've wondered what all this is about." A wicked smile came to Damion's lips, revealing his single gold tooth. "Let me show ya." He turned and marched toward the partition, disappearing behind the wall.

Fenlara listened to the shuffling in the next room. Something hit the ground and scattered. Pieces of over ripe fruit fell into view, rolling across the soggy floor. Something else went flying past the opening, crashing into the canvas wall, and a moment later her tormentor returned.

Damion was carrying a large leather satchel. The stitching was severely stretched and the sides were bulged to capacity. He took position in front of her and knelt down to open the flap.

Fenlara was taken back. She counted eight temporal batteries. The partially visible window of each one glowed a deep purple, near black. No explanation was needed. Her heart sank. If this man had drained eight dukes, what hope did she have of surviving this encounter? Moreover, how had he managed to trap so many? She could understand her own entrapment. She was still fairly new and lacked experience. Many of the others had been in service since the Wild Age. Hell, there was at least one from the Age of Immortals. How could someone so primitive damage their order so thoroughly?

"I see ya understand now." Damion's smile grew wide. He'd delivered a blow as powerful as any attack. "Each one of these containers has enough power to tear a hole into the realm of gods." He patted the satchel like a beloved child in his care. "Ya see, it's not enough to drain yer power. Once I've taken all that I can, I'm gonna destroy ya. I know the dukes only operate when he sleeps, and that means he's defenseless right now. Once I'm finished with ya, yer god is going to fall. There will be a new god of time, and those of us who helped him ascend will be his chosen few. We'll be gods among men. No longer will we have to hide in shadow and pick the scraps. It'll be a new age. An age where the undesirables are in charge. And there's nothing ya or yer pious order can do to stop it!"

Anger flooded her. It was one thing to threaten her life, but to threaten Ozmodius—that was a crime beyond redemption. With renewed focus, Fenlara pushed the bounds of her mind. The demonic grip was weaker than ever, though it's sway held over much of her abilities. Finding the hole she'd created, she reached through and took hold of her bindings. The ropes about her arms began to heat.

Damion leaned in close, his nose nearly touching her. "I'm gonna erase ya like yer kind have erased so many before!"

Hearing the final few strands pop against the tension, Fenlara lunged forward. The remaining ropes caught against her torso, halting her advance but it had been enough. Her forehead slammed into the rancid man's face. An echoing crunch rang out and Fenlara fell back against the post.

Chapter XIII

The dirt was unforgiving and painful. Fenlara sighed, pushing herself up once again. Wiping the clinging grit from her face, she spun, searching for her opponent. Another blow appeared out of nowhere and she was falling again. The swirling lights passed quicker than she could see, and a field of grain greeted her. Fenlara slammed face first into the golden stocks. "Damn it!"

"You have to forget how you fought as a mortal. Those tactics are no longer of use. They won't work in a battle of time. It's all about outsmarting your opponent. You have to think in multiple dimensions, planning several steps ahead. Rule of combat number two, anticipate your opponent. You must identify what they're going to do before they do it. Once you know their plan, change it to your advantage."

Another blow impacted from the dirt and Fenlara flew into the sky, falling in reverse. She crashed into a stone ceiling, halting her ascent. She stuck for the briefest moment, lodged between the broken rocks, though it didn't last long. She fell, slamming into the compressed clay of a cavern floor. Fenlara groaned, pushing herself up. "How am I supposed to get ahead when I don't have time to catch my breath?"

Trendal pivoted on his heel and leapt. Flipping out of sight, he landed behind her. "Do you expect your enemies to take it easy? Do you think they'll hesitate because you can't keep up?"

"No, I just—" Another temporal door opened and Fenlara fell into the timestream. She had to get ahead of this. If she could alter the destination, maybe she could interrupt the next attack. Clearing her mind, a plan began to take shape.

Fenlara selected her target, feeling the tunnel shift around her. She passed through the wall of energy, bracing herself for what was to come.

Water encapsulated her. Fish scattered, fleeing the unexpected visitor. Light was sparse. The undergrowth stretched their slimy appendages toward the surface, collecting what sustenance they could.

Fenlara searched her surroundings, wondering how much time she had before Trendal would be upon her. Rapidly, she applied her cantrips, making breath unnecessary. It was the same for her other limitations. She could move and see as well if not better than on land. Now all she had to do was plan her next action before Trendal found her.

It was too late. The elder duke appeared out of nowhere. A blast of energy exploded around her, forcing the water to flee the pocket of air.

Gasping, unable to breathe in the unfiltered air, Fenlara dispelled her cantrip, recognizing her mistake nearly as quick as she'd made it.

The wall of water came crashing down, filling the void with such force. Tumbling, thrashing, unable to breathe, unable to fight, Fenlara was surrounded. This wasn't working at all like she'd planned.

Opening her own temporal door, the duke in training dove in and began searching for a place she might have an advantage. She'd spent enough time with Trendal to know there wasn't much he couldn't handle. That didn't leave many options. But he'd also said she had to anticipate his actions. There was more to that than simply knowing what he was going to do next. Nodding her understanding, she rocketed forward and burst through the wall.

Her feet landed solid on grass. Instantly, she spun, readying her spell.

The doorway opened and Trendal casually stepped through.

This was her chance. Unleashing the gathered energies, a bolt flew from her hands and engulfed the pursuing duke. It wrapped around him, lifting him off the ground and carrying him backward several feet.

Trendal dropped from the cocoon, falling slowly toward the earth.

Fenlara watched her prison continue on, carrying a shell of energy that greatly resembled her mentor. She hadn't expected him to escape so easily. Time dwindling before he'd be upon her, she forced another spell to the forefront of her mind.

Hitting the ground at a sprint, Trendal charged, sword in hand. He advanced like the bullet they'd used for training so long ago, moving faster than she could see.

Preparing herself, Fenlara set the final piece of her trap. She'd learned how to stop the bullet. With any luck she could stop him just the same.

Just out of reach, Trendal lunged, sword aimed, ready to strike. It crossed into her range, but before it could strike, both it and he were gone.

Fenlara paused, searching for the duke. He hadn't fallen into her trap. He hadn't gotten close enough. Too late to respond, she caught movement out the corner of her eye. The sting of a razor-sharp edge bit into her neck, halting no sooner than it made contact. Frozen, Fenlara felt a trickle of blood escape the minor wound. She refused to move, uncertain what was to follow.

Trendal held the bastard sword outstretched, ready to end her at a moment's notice. A cocky smile formed upon his lips.

This was it. He had her. Fenlara knew he wouldn't strike, at least not lethally. But she was also painfully aware how much the body could endure. At the same time, doubt grew inside her. It was the gleam in his eyes. Something about it was unsettling. It made her question his intent, if only for a moment.

Trendal retracted the blade, lowering it to his side. "You have to remember, your enemies will not fight fair. In the game of life and death, the only goal is to survive by any means necessary."

He wasn't wrong. He never was. With that in mind, this was the perfect opportunity to strike. Fenlara spun, dropping her shoulder to guard against an untimely sword swipe. Her left hand extended out, releasing the gathered energies. It blasted the duke in the chest.

Trendal flew backward, landing hard. Chunks of dirt, grass, and rock exploded, raining down upon him. Coming to a stop, he stared up from the fresh crater, approval upon his face. He smiled, taking in the sight of the darkstone sword pointed at his throat. "Well played!"

Fenlara grinned, taking joy in the temporary victory, though it didn't last long. A hard impact knocked her legs from beneath her and she slammed into the ground. "That's cheating!"

"That's rule number one. Cheating is a term used by losers. We can't afford to lose." The duke sheathed his sword and extended a hand to pull her to her feet. "You have a way to go, but I think you've suffered enough today." Summoning his pocket watch, Trendal glanced at the time. "We have a job to do anyway."

Chapter XIV

Instinctively, Damion threw his hand over his face. Blood ran between his fingers and down his chin. "Ewe fuckin bitch! Yr're onna pay for dat!" Anger flooded him. Stepping forward, he raised his fist, prepared to strike.

Fenlara had hoped for this, though not necessarily the being beaten while confined part. She'd have to improvise there. It was the emotional response she'd hoped for. Emotions led to mistakes. All she had to do now was wait for the right mistake. Bracing herself, she prepared for the impact. To her surprise it never came.

Hurried footsteps rushed into the room and a mug of bubbly liquid hit the ground.

"Let it go, man. You can't say you didn't owe her at least that one!" The younger man stood between the two, restraining his companion's arms. "Take a walk and get yourself cleaned up."

Damn it! If ever there was a time she wished the young man was not present, it was now.

Damion glared, his hate filled gaze shifting from the imprisoned duke, to his companion, and back again. Gritting his blood lined teeth, he spat the red mucus onto the floor, threw his hands in the air and stormed out.

Fenlara listened to him mumble under his breath as he passed out of sight. Judging from the commotion outside, she was fairly certain he'd flipped a table in his rage.

The younger man approached the flap that made the outer door. Pulling it aside, he stole a glance and closed it once again.

Hurrying to the duke, he knelt before her, mindful of the distance. There was much she didn't know and he didn't have much time to explain it. "That wasn't an overly smart thing to do. He isn't the forgiving type. He's going to demand retribution, and I promise you it won't be pleasant."

Fenlara wanted to speak but the silence spell was certain to prevent it. She wasn't sure what to expect from this one. He'd been the voice of reason, sure. But he was working with time criminals. What was to separate him from the rest?

Reaching over, the young man closed the battery, stopping its absorption. "I don't expect you to trust me, just know I'm not here to harm you." His hand glided past her head, removing the needle lodged in the side of her neck. Inspecting the transparent tube, a chuckle escaped him. "I assume you did this?" He held it up for her to see.

Fenlara noticed the dark ichor within was clogged just short of the needle. The tube was charred and smashed shut, preventing its contents from flowing. She stared at it for a long moment. If she'd done it, it had to have happened just before she blacked out. All she wanted at that point was to stop the demon blood from poisoning her. It seemed her prayer was answered.

Drawing his dagger, he went to work cutting the ropes around her legs. It was the least useful place to start but he couldn't be sure she wouldn't lash out before he'd had a chance to explain himself. "My name is Earon Torcavious. I'm a cleric of Ozmodius under assignment." He paused, allowing her a moment to process the information.

"I infiltrated this group a little over two years ago. Back then they were little more than a cult calling themselves The Pendulum. It started small, the occasional theft, break in, or desecrated alter. We didn't worry much about them until they started kidnaping priests. One day a Duke Tarset showed up. He asked a few questions and disappeared. We never saw him again.

Over the next few months, The Pendulum grew in both reach and power. When I was assigned this task, I went looking for the priests, as well as the duke, but I never found them. Rumors began to circulate. I thought them boast at first, but then they managed to trap a duke. I couldn't do much to help him, but maybe I can help you."

Fenlara listened intently, awaiting the final bond to be cut. It was a compelling story but for all she knew it was just that. He could just as easily be part of the ploy. If she trusted him, what would it mean for her? Though logic spoke louder than her skepticism. What choice did she have? Certain death awaited her if she stayed. At least she'd have a fighting chance this way.

Working diligently, Earon severed line after line, working his way upward. Just a few more and she'd be free. "They can't have all this power. Once you're free, you need to use it to get out of here. Warn any who are left. Maybe, with Ozmodius' favor, we can shut this down before it gets any more out of hand." He snatched the satchel off the floor and tossed it in her lap.

Fenlara caught it roughly. Opening the flap, she grabbed hold of the first canister she saw. She was familiar with how they'd used it to drain her, but she wasn't certain how to reverse the process.

Digging his dagger into the final braid of twisted hemp, Earon sawed earnestly, watching the strands unravel. He was nearly through. Just a few more slices and the duke would be free.

A sickening pop preluded the rupture in his throat. The blade retracted, spurting crimson fluid from the lethal wound.

Fenlara watched the fading surprise in Earon's dulling eyes. He collapsed face first atop her legs, his body twitching in its final death throes. She stared at the back of his head, watching his life fluid spill onto her. She was stunned. He'd given everything to help her and she hadn't been able to do the same. She'd seen Damion approach. She wanted to scream out, to cripple him with her growing strength, but it had all happened so fast. He'd struck before she could warn him.

"I never liked that guy." Damion spat a mouthful of blood and saliva onto the corpse. His eyes locked on the duke, smiling his wicked vengeance.

Fenlara thrashed from side to side, struggling to break the final strands holding her. She flailed her arms, fighting to break free. If she didn't escape now, chances were she wasn't going to. The murderous villain had already proven his resolve. Fear grew inside her. She was powerless, unable to cry out, unable to pray. Certain death on the horizon pleading screams formed in her mouth, though the words refused to resonate.

An audible snap echoed. It took Fenlara a moment to register her bonds had broken. She was free, yet she couldn't run. Something held her, something she couldn't identify. Staring her rage at the man, whimpering cries echoed behind him. Her vision shot to the helpless girl lying on the floor. She was bound and gagged, but there was no mistaking that fiery red hair or those bright blue eyes.

Chapter XV

Fenlara found herself standing in waist deep water. A forceful wave washed ashore, threatening to cover her whole. The undercurrents pulled at her legs as the lapping water shoved her forward. Struggling to maintain her footing, the water began to recede. She didn't have much time before another wave would be upon her.

Drawing her temporal powers to the surface, the world came to a stop. Waves ceased their crash against the shore. Overhead birds paused midflight, unaware of the change around them. Even the wind that had been steady and firm held fast. Using her newly obtained abilities was becoming easier with each passing day. Most of the time she didn't even think about it anymore.

Fenlara pulled herself atop the water, her thick soles connecting firmly against the still and solid surface. It'd taken some time to learn the simple trick, but she'd discovered it on her own. Water needed time to be pliable. When time was denied, the surface tension was no different than that of stone. It made walking much easier, though it did little for her already soaked clothing. Wet clothes were sure to cause chafing. That certainly wasn't how she wanted to start her day. "Become a duke they said. It'll be fun they said. I miss my turnips!"

"Quit your bickering. You're the one who failed to select a dry place to land."

Fenlara's glare snapped to the duke standing not far from her on the shore. "I don't like you sometimes. Not sure I've said that yet."

"Pretty much every day for the past week. Maybe two. Just think, pretty soon you won't have to worry about my charming smile or sparkling personality." Trendal laughed and began walking the shore, avoiding the lingering water trapped near his feet.

Releasing an exasperated breath, Fenlara ran her hand from the back of her head, over her face, and down her body. Heat surrounded her, growing warmer by the moment. It was hot but not uncomfortable. Steam rolled from the damp clothing and disappeared almost instantly. Within a few moments she was completely dry, though several patches of white salt marred her otherwise onyx apparel.

"What do you think we're supposed to do here?" Trendal asked, kicking a piece of wood that had drifted ashore.

"I don't know yet. I don't think were in the right place." Fenlara glanced around. The disturbance had been so vividly clear. She was supposed to be on a ship, a flaming, severely damaged, and sinking ship, but a ship nonetheless. Why was she nearly drowning off the coast of some random island in the middle of the Reinir Sea?

"Look at it again. The answers aren't always the first thing we see. Search the background, pick out any details that may prove useful."

Fenlara placed her hand to the hourglass on her armor. Each duke had their own way of tracking abnormalities. For her, the symbol of her god was the one thing she'd always cherished most. Well that and her garden, but the garden wasn't easy to carry with her.

An image filled her mind. Flame and smoke billowed around her, its heat and licking appendages dormant in the still image. The forward mast was broken, held aboard only by taut rigging, though the fire would soon release it. The crew was dead, save for one. He was a stout man with bald head and a thick red beard, though the tone was not so bright as her own fiery hair. He'd been lashed to the main mast. His face was contorted somewhere between anger and sorrow, though Fenlara suspected it was a mix of the two. Whoever had arranged this had been thorough.

Turning her attention to the distance, she searched for any sign of land. She had to be on the island for a reason. If this man was supposed to survive, and that was exactly what was supposed to happen, perhaps it was this island where he would seek refuge. But where was it?

Squinting, a tiny speck caught her attention, far to the east. It was little more than a slight discoloration, hidden by ridges in the water's surface and the sun's reflective glare. Such a sight was nearly impossible to see through an artist's rendition. That was all a timestop was really, a moment in time where everything and everyone was frozen.

Quickly forcing her will into action, Fenlara's vision enhanced. Her sight flew over the water faster than she could move. Nearing the discoloration, she realized it was a bird diving after a fish. It wasn't much, but it was more than she had before. And it gave her a direction to search. If there was a bird, that meant land had to be nearby.

Releasing the vision, Fenlara walked to shore and released her stop. She could feel the buildup growing from holding it so long.

"Did you find anything?"

"I think so. I saw a bird far to the east." Circling, she located west. "If I'm correct, what we're looking for is that way."

"All right. Are you familiar with the truesight spell?"

"I used it a couple times during the last Demon War, but I don't know how that's going to help us here. It doesn't do much for things not hidden by magic."

"Patience, young grasshopper. I'm about to Mister Miyagi you."

83

"I have no clue what you're talking about."

"I know you don't. That's part of what makes it so fun." Trendal smiled as he approached. "You're a skilled cleric, and an exceptional psion, but you haven't paired the two magics much. And really, once you add in the influence of time, that's all being a duke is. I want you to create the truesight spell, but instead of asking for Ozmodius' blessing, do it using your psionic abilities."

"But—how am I supposed to—"

Trendal lifted his hand silencing her. "From where does the magic of your clerical abilities stem?"

"Ozmodius, of course."

"Incorrect! Ozmodius is your patron. It's through his grace your power works, but he is not the link. The link is just that, a link between the divine and the mundane. Without the link, neither side gets what they want. Now, where do you think your psionic abilities come from?"

"My mind."

"Again, incorrect. Psionics are controlled and augmented through the power of will, but their source is innate to your existence. Your psionic abilities come from you, your life force, your soul, they are as much a part of you as the skin and meat your body is composed of. And that means two things. One, your power is unique to you. No other psionisist has your unique signature, which means psionic abilities can be tracked to their caster. And second, you are your own power source. Now, imagine you are your own link. I want you to tap into your clerical abilities through your psionics."

"Isn't that a little close to blasphemy? I mean, if I were to become my own deity, complete with clerical abilities—It just seems like something Ozmodius wouldn't approve of."

"Do you intend on forsaking him as your patron and falling from his grace?"

"No!"

"Then you have nothing to worry about."

"I guess—It just feels a little wrong."

"What we do is in the service of Ozmodius. We are the protectors of our god. Sometimes that means using whatever we have at our disposal. If you don't wish to reach your full potential, I need to know now so I can stop wasting my time."

"No, I want to learn." Fenlara closed her eyes, forcing her will. It didn't take much to lock onto her own power but connecting the two was harder than she'd imagined. Summoning the necessary forces to cast the truesight spell, she began channeling.

"Okay, now that you're that far, I want you to forget the spell triggers and force it into being. Let your power blend."

It was a strange sensation. Fenlara could feel everything swirl together. She was fueling her own magics, but it was more than that. The temporal powers were enhancing the bond, generating a force she'd never felt before. Every thought was laid out, awaiting her approval. She was the master of her own mind. Nothing was beyond reach. Opening her eyes, Fenlara was surprised by her sight. Existence was clear. Solids were hollow, transparent even, but she could tell what they were. Magic lingered on surface and in the air. She could see what it was. Where it came from. How powerful the caster was.

Temperature ranged by color. Time had no meaning. The history of this island played out before her, as did its future. For lack of a better word, her sight was pristine. The only thing that scared her was Trendal. He was something she could not fully identify, but perhaps he was intentionally shielding himself.

"Good. Now, I want you to locate the ship."

Fenlara's sight soared into the sky as if under the duke's command. She was miles above the island, looking down. There was no surprise it was unsettled. No structures stood above the treetops, though that wasn't to say nobody lived there. The island's history played out in the blink of an eye. It told her everything and everyone who had ever visited. Hundreds of birds could be seen, some frozen midflight encircling their next meal, others were perched in the treetops or on the bluffs. There was nothing but water in every direction, spanning beyond the horizon. The island itself was the only land for nearly a month, consisting of mostly trees and a few rocky bluffs along the western edge.

Several hundred miles out, just over the horizon, smoke caught her attention. Fenlara was there in a moment's notice, floating above the burning construct. "I found it!"

"Good. Now release your sight and take us there."

Fenlara returned to her physical form, still reeling from the power coursing through her. She'd never felt anything so intoxicating. On instinct an orange glow wrapped around both her and the duke, blocking all sight for the briefest moment. When it faded, she found herself standing in the middle of the ocean. The waves were shallow, frozen on the glassy surface. It took conscious effort to realize she'd placed them in another timestop.

Not far from where she stood the three-mast schooner sat idle, half swallowed by sea. The sails were in ruin, much of the rigging burned away. The stern was completely submerged, and much of the bow ablaze.

"Good job. Just remember that power can corrupt. Don't allow yourself to fall victim to it." Trendal warned, casually approaching the burning ship.

Following her mentor, Fenlara approached the port side. At least she believed it was the port side. Her nautical terminology was somewhat lacking. She'd never been a sailor of any kind, though her previous career had taken her aboard a few ships when a long distance trip had to be made. Either way, it seemed silly that sailors had to have different names for everything. Left, right, port, starboard, even their miles were different from the standard. Shaking her head, Fenlara grabbed hold of some of the rigging and pulled herself up.

The waterline wasn't far from the main deck, and by extension, the main mast where her query was subdued. The details of her vision paled in comparison to seeing it for herself. She'd seen the bodies. It was nothing now that she was here among them. The sweet scent of blood and cooking flesh filled her nostrils, destroying what little appetite she had. A sea of red ran down the planks like tiny rivers, diluting when they reached the water. The bodies were splayed like trophies, each one in clear view of the red bearded man. This was a massacre, a message. Whoever had done this wanted to torment this man, this devonie, to the brink of insanity.

Fenlara had met a few of his kind during her travels. She found it odd she hadn't identified him as such earlier. Though had she not been familiar with his race, she would have simply thought him a man with the mannerisms of the dwarves. It mattered little. She was here to help regardless if he was man, dwarf, devonie, or something far more sinister.

Turning her attention to the slaughtered crew, she couldn't help but notice the sword slashes were exceptionally precise. They were meant to inflict the most amount of pain with the slowest possible, yet unescapable death. Yet not one of the victims had a weapon in hand or showed the slightest sign of defense. This attack happened fast, without warning. In fact, being a duke, she knew that was exactly what had happened. These men had been murdered and arranged under a timestop. She could feel the lingering energies of it. "Do you feel that?"

"I do. We have a chronomancer on our hands."

"What's that mean?"

"Someone who plays with temporal magic. It's usually a wizard who stumbles upon a time travel spell and decides to mess with things they don't understand. But no worries. Once we're done here, I intend to track them down and put a stop to it."

"I'd say whoever this devonie is, he's clearly made an enemy."

"That's putting it mildly."

Fenlara approached the bound man. Staring into his burning eyes, she could feel the pain inside him. It was unsettling. If she were to free him there was no doubt he'd attack on instinct, fueled by undiluted rage. Taking a step back, she inspected for any wounds.

His already red beard was saturated in blood, though it didn't appear to be his own. The gleam of his freshly shaven head reflected only the orange glow of the burning sails. A few embers had landed, blistering his flesh, but otherwise he appeared undamaged.

Fenlara cut the ropes securing him, making sure she didn't release him from the timestop. "He needs to be on the island for rescue. There's enough there to keep him alive until that happens. Do you mind grabbing one of those broken planks?"

"What for?" Trendal glanced to the shattered deck where the foremast had fallen. Most were already charred beyond use, but a few looked salvageable.

"If you've taught me right, we were never here. That means we have to make his survival believable, both to himself and everyone else. If you were in his position, would you believe you woke up on an island without so much as a piece of debris around you?"

"First off, I would never find myself in such a position. But you're right. Good job thinking ahead. I knew I found the right person for the job."

A smile escaped her. Pulling the stocky man's weight onto her shoulders, a groan escaped and Fenlara drug him forward a few steps. "He's heavier than he looks."

"That's why we use magic." Trendal taunted.

Fenlara's face contorted. "That's why we use magic." She mocked. Unleashing her power, the orange glow wrapped around them and they appeared just off the coast of the island. Releasing the man, she took the plank from Trendal and positioned it under him as best she could. He was close enough to swim the rest of the way. "I guess let's get out of here. I want to find this chrono guy and go get some of that Chinese food you told me about."

The Duke Target

Levi Samuel

Chapter XVI

Lifting the blood drenched blade, Damion glanced from the dripping fluid to the duke. "Ya know? In hindsight, he was right." He rotated the short sword, pointing the tip at the dead man in Fenlara's lap. "I should have killed ya sooner. No matter. I got what I wanted from ya, and I rooted out a traitor in the process. I think I'll consider that a win." Turning on heel, Damion wrapped his fist into the wild hair of the young woman behind him. Pulling her to her feet, he pressed the stained edge against her throat.

Fenlara took in the sight of the young woman, staring in stunned silence. Her eyes were puffy and bruised. She'd been beaten severely and held captive for gods knew how long. Fresh blood ran from a wound on her cheek, though it had crusted and dried in many places. Her clothes were stained and ripped, and a large chunk of hair was missing.

Pieces of the puzzle were flying through her mind, though she still lacked the full picture. None of this had been by accident. They'd trapped her here for a reason, a reason that she now knew. Fenlara stared into the bloodshot eyes of the frightened girl, the girl who would one day become a Duke Tarset. She was shocked by how much she'd grown since then. She was no longer the timid and overly sheltered cleric that stood before her. The girl who'd begrudgingly joined a band of heroes and marched headlong into the demon war. She'd come back from the war changed. The world had become a bigger and much darker place since she left the blackened halls of the temple. The girl before her hadn't yet experienced many of the tribulations that shaped her into who she would become, but it was undeniably her. She could feel it in her core. This was why she was here. They couldn't trap her elsewhere. They had to do it in a place forbidden to her. That was the only way to ensure no one came looking.

"I see ya understand now." Damion kicked the back of the girl's leg, dropping her to her knees. "I can't tell ya how long I've been waiting for this moment. I feared this one wouldn't survive long enough for ya to arrive."

That statement made no sense. If she'd been tortured for any length of time, the memories should have already transferred. Something wasn't right here. Fenlara paused. That was the understatement of eternity. Nothing here was right. It didn't change the fact that it was happening. The question was, how did she fix it without interacting with her younger self? Her temporal powers were depleted, and enough demon blood remained to make everything else unreliable. She couldn't rightly throw the asshole through a wall when he was holding a captive to whose fate she was bound. Even without the ropes, she had to face the fact, she was still a prisoner.

Turning her attention to the young girl, barely a woman, Fenlara felt remorse. Her decisions started this. She hadn't done anything directly, but she'd accepted the mantle. She'd become a duke. Despite all the precautions and protocols, a target had been placed on this girl's back long before she really had the chance to explore the world.

"What have you done?" The words flowed from her, though she hadn't meant to speak them. The break in silence seemed as much a shock to Damion as it was to her. That opened this up to a whole new level.

Recognizing the new danger, Damion burnished the sword, pulling the girl closer. "Shut yer damned mouth! Ya so much as utter another word and I'll kill her before ya can blink."

There were a few things Fenlara knew about negotiations. The first being communication was mandatory. If both parties didn't communicate, it was no longer a negotiation. Secondly, it was only a stalemate until the status quo shifted. Lastly, and probably most important, leverage was only useful until it was used. This put her in a difficult spot. She couldn't afford to let the leverage shift into collateral damage. But there was one detail Damion was forgetting. Prayer wasn't always spoken aloud.

Fenlara clutched the temporal battery she'd removed from the satchel. Silently praying to Ozmodius, she readied herself. Everything was going to move fast and she couldn't be certain the demon blood wasn't still blocking her.

Taking a deep breath, Fenlara exhaled slowly. In one fluid motion, she brought the canister back and flung it as hard and accurate as she could. It soared across the tent like a missile, hitting its mark.

Unprepared for the sudden impact, Damion stumbled backward releasing both his sword and his hold on the girl.

"Run!" Grabbing another battery, Fenlara pulled herself from beneath Earon's corpse and jumped to her feet.

Damion recovered in no time, drawing a dagger. Charging, he plunged it deep into the young doppelganger.

"No!" Fenlara's knees slammed into the muddy ground. All hope was lost. She'd failed. There was no escaping death now, despite how she tried. The woman before her had to survive if she was to become who she was. That option removed, it would only be a short time until she faded from existence.

Twisting the blade for good measure, Damion retracted and wiped it on the dying woman's tattered clothing.

Young Fenlara staggered and fell. The pool of blood grew larger by the moment, soaking into the earth. Her skin was paling and turning blue. She blinked rapidly, tears running down her face. Helpless, she stared at her older self, unable to give voice to the words on her tongue.

Damion stepped over his dying victim, snatching up the satchel of batteries. Grabbing the one on the table, he paused, looking down at the defeated duke. "So ends the Duke Tarset!" Smiling, he turned away from her and made for the tent flap. She was no longer a threat. Soon she wouldn't even exist.

Chapter XVII

Chaotic forces ripped her this way and that, though it wasn't nearly as violent as she'd imagined. It had been the initial entry that was the hardest. Now that she was past the swirling wall, it was actually quite calm. The eye of the storm, she suspected.

Fenlara turned, glancing at what remained of the Hall of Guardians. The walls had been sundered, much of the rubble having been swept away. All that remained were a few pieces of the jagged foundation and her room, broken but holding strong. She somehow felt it was a metaphor for her resolve.

Hearing the voices, echoing through the roar of wild energies, Fenlara turned away. There was nothing further she could do for the unconscious girl trapped within her room.

The floor was surprisingly solid, despite being empty. There was no stone, nor wood, nor granite, or any other material that had so often comprised the ground in Purgatory. There was nothing but a swirling gray mist upon which her steps fell.

Much of the space between all spaces was uncharted. It served as a sort of way station in transition from one place to another. Most who came here didn't choose where they entered, though there were a few settlements within, like the Hall of Guardians, that maintained frequent traffic. In truth, one could spend their entire existence within Purgatory and never truly explore its vastness. Of course, it was hard to map something without landmarks.

Following the sound, Fenlara could see a crack just ahead. It was jagged, arcing across the nothing like a bolt of lightning trapped in stasis. The swirling storm crashed into its edges, breaking ever so slightly, creating a turbulence that would be difficult to cross. In the center, she could see a wide gap displaying somewhere else. It was the place, she recognized, through her window. The place where time had blended.

Nearing the crack, warm air rushed to greet her. She'd been sucked from her shelter. It stood to reason this last place in time was being sucked here as well. Straining against the force, Fenlara fought her way through the currents. The energies wrapped around her, though she was surprised to find they weren't attacking. If anything, they seemed to be aiding her, carrying her toward her goal. The power washed through, mixing with those she'd absorbed. They were protecting her. She was one with the paradox, the origin of it.

Eyes glowing, teeming with magic, Fenlara marched through the hole in reality and stepped into this new place that didn't exist before. She could hear the chanted words in the air, though they were foreign, of a language she'd never heard. Lightning sparked with her every movement, crackling between her fingers, dancing around her body. She was unstoppable.

The roaring storm became distant, nearly nonexistent. Fenlara didn't have to look to know the crack had sealed. She could feel it. That opened a world of possibilities. If she'd closed this rift, was it possible to close the others and fix all that had been broken? She didn't know, but she had to try.

Staring over this strange, yet oddly wonderful conglomeration before her, she was taken back by its unique wonders. She was on the mountain side overlooking what could have been one of any number of cities, though it was not of her time.

Towering buildings of stone and glass shot into the sky. Many of them had collapsed into heaping piles of rubble and dust. In the distance a dragon circled overhead, raining fire upon all in its path. An ear shattering roar escaped the creature, sending rubble tumbling down into the streets. She'd never met a red before but their reputation labeled them as particularly nasty. The shattered streets themselves were lost to a chaos of their own. Despite the jagged stone and overturned vehicles, pedestrians fled for whatever safety they could find. An army of orcs and alfar waged war, slaughtering any in their wake. Gunshots and sirens echoed. The sky was filled with holes, drawing the rolling clouds into space and the void beyond.

Fenlara glanced into the sky, locating the source of a buzzing hum that lingered in the air like static. It began as a shadow beyond the clouds. Lights flickered just out of sight, and a moment later a huge metal boat broke the surface. Down it continued, crashing into many of the large buildings. Fire and stone and ash scattered from the wreckage. Another boat chased, raining blasts of red and green light upon the first.

The dragon swirled around, its gargantuan leathery wings flapping to carry it higher. A billow of flame rolled from its snout, showering the metal in an orange glow. The reptile was dwarfed by comparison, but the chromatic dragons were known to be extremely territorial and not afraid of much. If it had claimed this city, this chaos, perhaps it considered the flying contraption competition.

Fenlara watched the spectacle, uncertain where to begin.

The damaging lights erupted from the now flaming boat, impacting the great beast. A roar of pain echoed like thunder. Chunks of scale and meat and bone fell from the sky. The creature tumble downward, much of its torso blown out. It landed abruptly atop one of the few standing buildings, the sharpened needle at the top impaling it.

Turning her attention to the flying craft, Fenlara couldn't help but wonder who or what was onboard. Likely elves. It seemed oddly fitting to have elves in space, though in truth, it could have been any manner of creature. She hadn't navigated that time enough to claim any familiarity with it, Regardless, whatever she'd walked into, this was by far the worst massacre she'd ever seen.

"We need to fix this!" Fenlara announced, approaching the duke at the cliff's edge. Now that she was upon him, she knew his face, though they'd only met once before. Of the current dukes, Teddy had been in service the longest, at least next to Trendal. Nobody really knew when her mentor had accepted the mantle, though it was rumored he was among the first.

Seemingly surprised by the company, Teddy turned to face the young duke. "I thought all the others were dead. How'd you get here?"

"I caught a paradox." Her statement was more accurate than he would ever know, though she found humor in it. The hour was late and she wasn't sure how many more chances she'd get to make a joke.

Shaking his head, a look of regret fill Teddy's eyes. "They had one job to do, one!" He extended a single finger. Exhaling sharply, he sprang into action launching a blast of energy at the unsuspecting duke.

She felt the blast long before the attack registered. Flying back, Fenlara slammed into the jagged wall of rock. She bounced and hit the ground. A rumble echoed beneath her. She rolled just as an avalanche of blocks tumbled down. The castle's outer wall had collapsed from her impact. If she didn't move, it would bury her in seconds.

Teddy leapt, drawing his bastard sword and bringing it down in one fell swoop. The blade impacted the blackened armor of the prone Duke Tarset. It rung out with a crack of thunder.

Surprised her armor held, Fenlara rolled, avoiding a secondary blow. She'd given him too many free swings. Harnessing the powers coursing through her, she launched into the sky in an explosion of rock and dust. Her sword appeared in her hand as if it had a mind of its own. She knew the day for its use was coming but she never could have imagined it would be under such circumstances. Landing hard, the stone beneath her cracked, and her blade whipped around just in time to parry an incoming slash.

It was time to apply what Trendal had taught her. She needed to level the playing field and tilt the odds to her favor. Gathering her will, Fenlara opened a doorway into the timestream. There weren't many, if any, places left to go. Most had been destroyed by the paradox. It didn't matter where she went, all she needed was to gain the advantage.

A firm yank ripped her from the swirling chaos and Fenlara slammed face first into the rocky ledge. She clawed at the ground, trying to get to her feet. Why hadn't she gone anywhere? Even if this was the last point of existence, she still should have traveled a short distance. Never before had anyone stopped a time hop once it was started.

"You stupid girl. There's nowhere left to run. This is the last place before the complete destruction of Purgatory. After that Panthum is all that remains." Teddy stood near her feet, his sword raised, ready to deliver the final blow.

Fenlara watched it fall. She had to act now or it would all be over. Recalling Trendal's advice, the young duke brought her foot up, kicking as hard as she could. It was a cheap shot, but there was no such thing as cheating when death was on the line.

Teddy doubled over, abandoning his strike. His hands cupped his growing and he moaned, cursing the unexpected pain.

It didn't last long, but it bought her the time she needed. Fenlara launched herself over the cliff, using her overcharged abilities to stabilize her. She wasn't flying in the traditional sense. Rather she was falling with the absence of gravity, using minute bursts of energy to direct her. That was the only benefit to everything being connected at this one place. The known laws of physics didn't apply when the world was unstable. Hovering a few feet out, Fenlara knew what she had to do. She was a duke. She had to fix this as best she could. "Teddy, Duke Tarset of the Second Order, you have been found guilty of tampering with time and must pay the consequences. Surrender now and I will see you have a fair trial, to be judged by your peers. Deny and you will suffer the wrath of time!" It wasn't an official speech by any means, but it made her feel good.

"Ha! I have no peers. All of you are beneath me! I am Itish, bred for the sole purpose of destroying the gods, and they will feel my wrath!" Teddy launched himself toward her, his sword outstretched and aimed to run her through.

Fenlara spun, avoiding the blow. Of course, he wasn't going to come quietly. He didn't believe he was beaten yet, but there was one detail he was forgetting. She'd been trained by Trendal. She was thinking ahead. There were only a few options he could take that would alter the course, and she'd already identified them. Between that and the raw temporal energy coursing through her, she was no more than four steps from victory.

Realizing he'd missed, Teddy arched around and squared off once again. He'd come too far to let this girl interfere with his plans. Drawing a temporal battery from the ether, he twisted the top and pulled it open. Energy crackled around it, jumping from the device and into his body.

Silently cursing herself, Fenlara went to work calculating her next actions. She hadn't thought about the canisters. She'd believed them all empty, though in hindsight that was a stupid belief. She recalled one of Trendal's adages about eggs and baskets. Still, it didn't change much. The stolen magics were nothing compared to what course through her. Paradox power was raw and pure. It was unpredictable, which made it hard to control but it was all she had. Summoning her will, using her own link to fuel the spell, a wide smile came to her lips. Rule three whispered in her mind. *When all else fails, taunt your enemy into action.*

It worked. Teddy charged, his sword aimed to decapitate. She'd hesitated too long. There was no possible way she could avoid his blow before it landed. Slamming into her, confusion filled his mind. His sword passed straight through, though not to the effect he'd intended.

Fenlara hadn't moved. she'd refused to. The corrupt duke had cut straight through her. Her mock smile shifted, becoming one of victory. He'd stumbled straight into her trap. All that was left was to close it.

Teddy hacked, thrust, and slashed at the army of Fenlaras appearing around him. Despite his efforts, his sword was unable to purchase. He'd hit one only to have two others take its place. They closed in, constricting. Each time he made contact another would spawn, surrounding him.

Floating far overhead, Fenlara watched the spectacle. Hundreds of copies swarmed, locking themselves around him. They engulfed, tightening their grip. A flash of light erupted and the army became a solid cocoon of energy imprisoning the traitorous duke. Fenlara felt the last of the raw power leave her, funneled into the prison. If it couldn't hold him, nothing could. Exhaustion crept into her. Her eyes began to close. She felt like she was falling, though she lacked the strength to do anything about it. Clinging to her last sliver of consciousness, a prayer escaped her lips. "Ozmodius, my god, the traitor has been captured. Please fix this, for I do not have the strength."

The Duke Tarset

Levi Samuel

Chapter XVIII

Groggily, Fenlara came to. She was comfortable, protected. Opening her eyes, she saw a familiar face staring down at her. "Trendal?"

"I'm here."

"What happened?" Realization hit her and she shot up. "Teddy! He betrayed us."

"Shh. We know. He's been dealt with. Good job in capturing him, by the way. You used what tools you had at your disposal to get the job done. Not many would have been so resourceful. If I haven't said it before, I'll say it again. I knew I found the right girl for the job."

Fenlara fell back. Her strength was far from returned, though she was pleased to see she was in her own bed. That at least meant the Hall of Guardians hadn't been completely destroyed. "You have." A weak smile came to her. "Did everything get fixed?"

"Yes. It took quite a bit of effort to stop the paradox and revert its damage, but we managed."

"And the dukes? Teddy was draining them."

"All resolved. The temporal batteries have been collected and moved to a more—secure location. Rest now. You can give your formal report once you've recovered."

"What about me?"

"What about you?"

A shallow laugh escaped the young duke. It hurt more than she'd expected. "I made the paradox and brought an earlier version of myself here. Where is she?"

"She's had any memory of those events erased and has been returned to her own time. Though you don't have to worry too much about her. That sigil on your ribs will prevent any of this from ever happening again."

"How?"

"Let's call it an insurance policy. For lack of better understanding, she will continue to live her life as intended, as will you. Though her fate is no longer linked to yours. Rest now. There will be time for answers later. And congratulations. You've been promoted to Duke Tarset of the First Order. I have but one question for you. Do you still think the job is boring?"

Her head shook before the words could form. "No. Difficult and exhausting. And at times a little tedious. But I wouldn't describe it as boring."

Chapter XIX

Gentle rays of sunlight cascaded across a golden field of wheat. Running her hand across the fragile stocks, Fenlara smiled. It brought her to the days when things were simple. Back to a time not so long ago, when the world made sense. But all that was behind her now. The solace she'd strived so hard for had finally been achieved. That alone made it a good day.

Placing one foot in front of the other, the cleric casually made her way across the fertile land, keeping an eye to the horizon. The sun was on the decline. Only a few hours remained until it would disappear for the evening. So long as it remained at her back, she'd make it in time.

Following the remnants of a long abandoned farm road, Fenlara paused at the hilltop overlooking Winstead. It seemed much smaller than she remembered. The once bustling city was always busy with travelers and traders from the surrounding towns and villages. And of course, everyone came to pay homage at the Temple of Ozmodius. It was the temple that made the city. Its onyx pillars stretched into the sky, towering over everything around it.

So long it had been since she'd seen it, though time was merely an illusion. What had felt like decades in the moment had been a little over two years to the outside world. The threat of constant battle often had that affect.

Fenlara's fiery hair whipped about her face triggering a flood of pleasant and comfortable memories from the fair-sized settlement less than a mile in the distance. She'd finally made it.

After all she'd seen. After all she'd endured, she was finally home. A heartening smile came to her lips and she started her trek down the hill. It didn't take long to intersect the main road running through the city's heart. Unlike the former, this one remained heavily traveled and well maintained.

Approaching the watch tower at the city's edge, two guardsmen snapped to attention, offering salute to the cleric of Ozmodius.

Fenlara nodded her appreciation and continued past. As familiar as this city was, she was now a stranger to it. She hadn't been gone that long, but her world view had shifted drastically since her departure. She'd faced demon hordes, soulless prisoners, rogue wizards, and her fair share of criminals since the last time she walked these streets. The people of this world weren't as good as she'd always imagined. That wasn't to say they were all bad. If anything, she'd learned the world was not split between solid lines of good and evil. Much of it was comprised of shades between. She herself had been forced to make such decisions while she was away. Sometimes there was no good answer, simply the best you could do at the time.

The cleric passed by many homes and shops. The people didn't seem to pay her much mind. Of course, she was just another cleric here. They'd show respect if direct interaction was required, but little else would transpire. It wasn't like many of the outlying villages and outposts she'd visited in recent history. Most of them hadn't seen a cleric in ages. It often took her multiple days to tend to all of their spiritual needs. In more cases than not, she hadn't had that long. But it didn't mean she turned her back on them. She was a cleric. It was her duty to help the people as best she could. Clinching her journal, packed full of places and people who needed her attention, she fully intended to file a request for the missionaries to return in her stead.

Reaching the temple, Fenlara made her way up the multiple black steps and to the grand doors at their crest. Inspecting them, she said a silent prayer and approached. The large doors were too heavy to open from the outside. It required the High Priest's word, given only on special occasion. Instead, most used the small single person door carved seamlessly into the blackened stone. Squeezing her hand into a fist, the cleric gave a firm rap against the solid surface.

It rang out louder than a wooden door of the same size and a crack appeared where nothing had been moments before. It widened and within a few heartbeats the door was fully open to her.

"Priestess Fenlara, it's good to see you again." The priest gave a low bow showing his respect. "We heard news of the massacre at Stowcroft. Thank Ozmodius you survived that dreadful encounter."

"Thank you, Brother Modaeis. I was one of the fortunate ones that day. Ozmodius watches out for all."

"That he does, Sister."

Awaiting entry, a long uncomfortable moment passed. The priest apparently hadn't realized he was keeping her. Balancing on her heels, Fenlara broke the silence. "Brother Modaeis, do you mind if I have a word with the High Priest? I need to report in."

"Oh, my apologies, Sister." He chuckled to himself and stepped aside.

Fenlara entered the temple. Towering statues stood along the side walls, six to the left and six to the right, their swords drawn before them, hands resting in wait upon the hilts. No facial detail was discernable on any of them, though not for lack of feature. They had that in abundance. It was more aptly an overload. Each time one face would settle, another would take its place, keeping any observer from ever identifying the smallest detail. And they never repeated, at least not as far as anyone could tell.

For the most part, everything was the same as it had been the day she left. Even the dripping tails hanging from the candles appeared no different. A few members of the clergy were hard at work, sweeping the central chamber. The acolytes aided where required, tending their various duties, though most of the clergy was elsewhere. This was the largest temple within a month's travel by horseback in any direction. It housed nearly thirty devout followers at any given time and looked after over two hundred children from all walks of life. Most were simply busy elsewhere.

Navigating the corridors, Fenlara found her way to the High Priest's chamber. Knocking gently, she heard footsteps on the other side. The door swung open, revealing an old man dressed in black robes. A golden hourglass hung from an equally golden braid around his neck. Despite the wrinkles and discoloration of his skin, his eyes held a youthfulness unseen in most his age.

"High Priest Jerein, I've returned from my assignment. I'm happy to report the demon forces have been pushed back and banished from this world. May Ozmodius see they never return." Fenlara gave a deep bow, greatly exaggerated compared to that of Modaeis moments before.

"Please rise, Sister Fenlara, and come in. There's someone here who wishes to speak with you." Jerein stepped to the side, pulling the door open for her to pass. No sooner than she was clear, he stepped out and pulled the door closed behind him.

Fenlara watched the High Priest leave the room. This was not what she was expecting, though she had no idea as to what she had expected in the first place. Glancing about the room, she was curiously alone.

Only the High Priest's belongings were present. His canopy bed rested near the far wall. Grand and elegant robes of black, gold, and white were displayed from a stand in the corner. A writing desk sat near the center of the room, vellum piled high along one side and a quill resting atop a single piece at the center. The pooled ink beneath the tip was still glossy and wet. Several shelves were pressed against the walls, overflowing with books of all shapes, sizes, and colors.

Fenlara wanted to inspect the books. The temple had a fully stocked library with almost any book you would ever want to read. Why were there so many here, hidden from the world? Nonetheless, she had to show self-discipline. This was not a place to go snooping, despite her desires.

"Greetings." A familiar and youthful voice echoed behind her.

The cleric turned to find a man dressed in black armor made from a material unlike any other. An hourglass was carved into the left breast, specks of sand rising from the lower bulb and settling in the top. His hair was of a golden brown, paired with near flawless skin that nearly sparkled in the light. She knew this man. He'd come to her during her travels, offering advice when the path was unclear. Who was he, this man who had aided her so much? During their encounters he'd refused to give his name. The Demon Wars were over. The gateways had been closed. Why was he here now, after everything she'd been through, why was he so important to warrant a private audience within the High Priest's personal chambers?

An amused smirk came to his lips. "I can see you're confused. I don't blame you. I'm sure were our roles reversed I would be too."

"What are you doing here?" That wasn't the question she wanted to ask. It was simply the first to escape her. Fenlara studied him, searching for answers, hoping he'd provide more than his usual cryptic statements.

"I've come to extend you an offer. Have you heard of the Duke Tarset?"

A scoff escaped before she could stop it. "I don't know of a cleric who hasn't heard such myth. They're powerful warriors who serve Ozmodius as guardians of time. The stories are in abundance but there's no record of them anywhere, at least not beyond the church."

The dark armored man nodded in agreement. "There's no record because we don't exist. We don't exist because we can't. It's the only way to ensure time will remain unaltered by our actions."

"You keep saying we. You're telling me you're a Duke Tarset?"

"Duke is fine, and yes. My name is Trendal Torcavious. Left hand of Ozmodius, Duke Tarset of the First Order." He gave a subtle bow before continuing. "We dukes are few in number but our presence is felt throughout all of time and space. Without us, the world cannot function. Without us, Ozmodius cannot rest."

"Why are you telling me this?"

A mild chuckle escaped the duke. "We want you to join us. I'm asking you to become a duke. I understand much of what this means is beyond your current comprehension, but by accepting this role you'll serve Ozmodius in a station far beyond anything you could possibly hope to accomplish here." Trendal gestured to the world around them, dismissing the grand tapestries and effects as if they were little more than worthless dust.

An awkward pause filled the air. After a long moment of silence, Fenlara bounced on the heels of her feet and spoke. "So, you're like the most powerful duke?"

He chuckled. "In a sense. My status is no different than any other, though being of the First Order grants me command when cooperation is needed. Much of what we do is independent, but occasionally joint efforts are required."

"I see. So, what does a duke do? I mean aside from the time warden stuff?"

"As a duke you'll experience true freedom. You'll be unrestricted by age, power, even the time which you protect.

You'll visit lands far and near, some with magics and technologies beyond your current understanding. You'll bear witness to strange and wonderful things. Without limits you can experience thousands of lifetimes, each one teeming with knowledge and adventure. And when you've had enough, when you're ready to quit, the retirement package will see you never want for anything in this life or the next. You'll have a chance to start over. To live whatever life you desire, without worry or care."

"It sounds boring." Fenlara stated flatly.

"Boring?" Trendal cocked his head as if he didn't understand the statement.

"The retirement. Life without conflict would be boring." She stopped herself realizing what she'd just said. She'd spent much of her life within the temple, never desiring to visit the world outside its walls. She'd become complacent with a miniscule existence, never knowing adventure or excitement beyond that of mass. It all seemed so dull compared to the action she'd faced over the past two years. Sure, much of it had been dangerous. And she'd spent a fair amount of it afraid of what might happen the day after. But she knew she was alive. She couldn't say the same for her life within the temple. Taking a deep breath, Fenlara knew her decision was made. Nodding to herself more than to the duke, she looked up and smiled. "I'll do it. I'll become a Duke Tarset!"

The Duke Tarset

Levi Samuel

Epilogue

Anger was the only emotion that could describe what he was feeling. It was an anger well deserved. They were trespassing. Violators in his domain. Such an infraction would be paid in blood.

He glanced up, seeing the red beast soar overhead, twisting between two of the large buildings. The heat from its breath would boil the flesh of anyone it touched, but not him. He was immune to such.

Elves and orcs fought all around him, though most were too fearful to approach. It was smart of them. They knew better. The people, the humans, lost in this madness, unfamiliar with such displays weren't so enlightened. His daggers dripped with their blood. It wasn't that he desired their deaths. Simply that they'd come too close. They'd sought his protection. But protection was not his duty. Not when these trespassers were running rampant.

A crash echoed, shaking the streets and shattering windows. The dragon met its demise atop one of the buildings, though it was clearly dead before impact. That didn't stop the remaining starship from continuing to fire upon it.

He leapt into the sky, flying higher than the others could perceive. His booted feet landed on the hull, echoing a hollow tune. That was good. It meant he could get inside. Flipping his daggers, energy sparked around the enchanted blades and he plunged them deep into the metal, dragging them together. An energy field flickered and fell away, unable to guard against his perceived primitive attack. If only they knew what he was truly capable of. Retracting his blades, he slammed his foot into the incision, bending the metal to open a hole.

He stepped inside, falling a great distance to the interior floor. His brown leather duster flowed behind him like a cloak of death, trailing his every movement. The tendrils atop his head searched for his target, slithering like snakes of red and blue. The holes of his golden face revealed deep penetrating eyes, thirsting for blood, curious to absorb the world around them.

He landed without much of a sound, kneeling to absorb the blow and stepped from it as if it had been nothing more than a minor drop. He could feel his targets frolicking about, unaware of his presence. All they knew was something was wrong. Each one had been marked, unwittingly awaiting their deaths. The silver bells didn't lie. He didn't lie.

He searched the deck, drowning his blades in blood. Not a soul would survive his wrath. Making his way from corridor to room, room to corridor, he destroyed everything and everyone he found, the bells calling to him all the while.

Returning to the ground took little more than a thought. The scrapes and groans of destruction were joyous music to his ears. He stared at the falling starship, watching it smash into the towering buildings, toppling them with ease.

Power drew his attention to the mountains beyond the out of time city. He knew a pair of dukes when he saw them. He'd been present when Ozmodius had willed them into existence. But these were unknown to him. If not for his fondness for their god, he would have enjoyed watching them bleed out. They were trespassers on his domain, after all.

He was upon them in the blink of an eye, though neither would know of his presence. Listening to the bells jingling from their persons, he watched their battle. It was vastly unimpressive, though both were wielding power far beyond their station. That was the only thing that kept his interest. Though their lack of understanding was rapidly growing dull. At any time either could have decimated the other, but they drew it out, lingering in their battle far longer than was required.

This was boring. With a thought, he appeared on the outskirts of the city. In a few moments it would return to its proper place and he didn't wish to be stranded away from it. Time wasn't his domain and stealing a ride was harder than it sounded. Besides, the female duke was marked. She'd need time to recover before he exploited her services.

Straddling the iron frame, his foot kicked down on the lever and the engine roared to life. It was a low rumble that would terrify those unfamiliar with it, and he liked that. Kicking his duster from beneath him, he positioned himself into the pan seat and squeezed the clutch. Dropping into first gear, he let out slowly and twisted the throttle. Raked front forks stretched far ahead of him, the wide rear tire gripped the road behind. A small bronze jester's head dangled from each of the handlebars, dancing in the wind. His duster flowed behind him, narrowly avoiding the exposed rubber drawing into the pointed fender.

Working through the gears, he leaned, turning onto a dust covered road through the desert. Tumbleweeds rolled in the breeze, afraid to enter his path. He was chaos incarnate and nothing would challenge him.

Disappearing in the distance, a low echoing laughter faded with the roar of the motorcycle.

The Duke Target

Levi Samuel

Author's Notes

I created this book as a way of saying thank you to my readers. I couldn't do what I love without those of you who have supported me along the way. It takes a special sort to be there through thick and thin. I hope the story within these pages is adequate compensation.

I've noticed that each book I write seems to be harder than the last. That often leaves me claiming that 'This was the hardest book I've ever written.' In a way that statement holds true, though I've come to realize it's for different reasons than I initially suspected.

As I continue to grow and develop my craft, I'm experiencing techniques and methods of writing previously unknown to me. It seems the further down this career path I travel, the more rules I must adhere to. It's hard to write freely when you're so concerned with making mistakes. At a certain point you have to say screw it and just write the story. It can always be fixed later.

I learned that with this book. And while it was hard to wrap my head around the concept, I feel I'm closer to my goals, and therefore better because of it.

In a sense, this book was an experiment for me. I did something I've never done before. I broke almost every rule of writing I've ever been taught. But I didn't do so senselessly.

I wrote this book six different times. It didn't seem to matter how I approached I couldn't get it to agree with me. I spent numerous restless nights slaving over my laptop, pumping out words in the hope that something would click.

Finally, one night, I was laying on my cot trying to fall asleep. A sea of thoughts, memories, and ideas raced through my head, hindering my desire, when suddenly something sparked. I knew what I had to do.

The previous tellings of this story fell flat. I didn't know how to blend the various moods I felt justified the characters within. Fenlara is a quirky, quick-witted, turnip obsessed nerd who randomly spouts off useless trivia and random movie quotes. But she's also a badass warrior who blends magics in the defense and service of her god. Provided you read the book, you'll see I achieved much of that goal, though I couldn't always have her the one making puns.

For the trials and tribulations of her story, post Demon War, I had to have a somewhat dark plot. I was struggling trying to find ways to immerse this overly light character into darkness without extinguishing her light, and have it remain somewhat believable.

I thought what better way to accomplish this in a time travel book than by including some wibbly wobbly, timey wimey stuff.

The story happens chronologically, but the moods were wrong. It was all light, or it was all dark. I had to blend the two. And I managed this by following a fairly strict formula. By jumping so frequently between current, past, and flashback past settings, I was able to deliver a story that played to the mood, while tying together comprehensively. At least that was the intention. I trust you'll let me know if I failed.

That said, I hope you enjoyed the book. If so, please check out the others in my Eldarlands Saga if you haven't already done so. It's a large world, full of hundreds of characters, stories, and plot twists that I'm slowly getting out there a book at a time.

Thanks for reading. I humbly ask you to spare a few moments more by leaving me a review with your online retailer or choice. Reviews help turn a nobody author into a successful author.

Levi Samuel
July 2019

CPSIA information can be obtained
at www.ICGtesting.com
Printed in the USA
LVHW080231090121
675671LV00044B/476